A Fiction Lover's Devotional

21 Days of Christmas

Stories that Celebrate God's Greatest Gift

BroadStreet
PUBLISHING

Published by BroadStreet Publishing Group, LLC
Racine, Wisconsin, USA
www.broadstreetpublishing.com

21 Days of Christmas

Stories that Celebrate God's Greatest Gift

ISBN: 978-1-4245-5051-7 (hardcover)
ISBN: 978-1-4245-5052-4 (e-book)

Cover design by Chris Garborg at www.garborgdesign.com
Typesetting by Katherine Lloyd at www.TheDESKonline.com

Stock or custom editions of BroadStreet Publishing titles may be purchased in bulk for educational, business, ministry, fundraising, or sales promotional use. For information, please e-mail info@broadstreetpublishing.com

Printed in China

15 16 17 18 19 20 5 4 3 2 1

Contents

Introduction

The Christmas season, more than any other time of year, is known for its cherished traditions. Let me share some of mine with you.

Coming up with clever gift ideas for friends and family, then fighting crowds at the mall, scouring catalogs, and surfing the Internet to find them.

Belting out my favorite carols in the car as I drive to the grocery store to pick up the ingredients I need to make special goodies I never indulge in any other time.

Hauling out the bins stored in the guest-room closet so I can decorate the house, inside and out. Smiling at the memories triggered by nostalgic ornaments as I hang them on the tree.

Traveling "over the river and through the woods" to go from sunny California to snowy Colorado to enjoy a white Christmas with my family.

Attending Christmas services at church—especially those that end with everyone singing "Silent Night" a cappella in a candlelit sanctuary.

Watching a miniature Mary and Joseph reenact the nativity, complete with toddler angels, shepherds, and barnyard animals. Getting misty eyed at the children's choir performance, yet holding back a grin when one little girl sings just a bit off-key and louder than everyone else, and one little boy spends his entire time on stage adjusting his collar.

And finally, reading heart-warming classics like "Twas the Night Before Christmas" and Dr. Seuss's *The Grinch Who Stole Christmas.* And of course the story of Jesus' birth from the book of Luke … which Linus recites so beautifully in *A Charlie Brown Christmas.*

Whatever traditions you enjoy this year, I hope you'll take a few moments out of your busy holiday schedule to read the stories in this book. A few are fictionalized accounts of what Mary and Joseph must have gone through in that little town of Bethlehem on that oh-so-holy night. Most of the stories are about people like you and me, searching for meaning and purpose during this season of love, peace, and good will.

As you get caught up in these inspiring tales, and find yourself relating to the characters and their situations, I pray that your heart will overflow with comfort and joy. And with the source of true comfort and joy: *Jesus.*

—Kathy Ide

1

Christmas Then and Now

by David B. Carl

June yanked the seat belt so hard it locked in place. Taking a deep breath to calm her nerves, she let it retract, then forced her arm to move slowly across her body before clicking the metal tab in place.

Norm pulled out of the driveway, a scowl on his haggard face. "They've probably started without us."

"I hope they have. Why should their dinner be ruined just because we're late?" She leaned over the center console and glared at her son and daughter in the backseat. "You kids are being careful with that Jell-O salad, aren't you?"

Sally nodded, her eyes wide. But Billy ignored her, doodling on the foil with his thumbnail.

June turned back to her husband. "Norman, your son is drawing designs on the foil over my Jell-O salad."

Her husband maneuvered a right turn without looking back. "Billy, get away from that salad this instant or I'll make you wish you'd never—"

June gasped. "You shouldn't talk to the children that way."

Norm took a long breath. "Snuggle Bunny," he cooed, "if it's all right with you, would you mind not playing too much with the aluminum foil on your mother's Jell-O salad?"

June punched him in the arm for the thousandth time in their marriage.

"Ow!"

Mary reached for the water bag hanging from the donkey's saddle, but stopped short when a piercing pain crossed her abdomen. "Ooh!"

Joseph, who'd been walking alongside her, stopped abruptly. "Are you all right?"

She sent him what she hoped was an assuring smile. "Oh, yes. I just moved wrong." She reached again, but another pain hit. "Oh!"

Joseph pulled a smoothly polished wooden cup out of the saddlebag, poured some water, and handed it to her.

"Thank you." She took a sip, then handed him the cup. "Do you expect Bethlehem to be very crowded?"

He frowned. "More than I wish it would be."

"Do you think we'll have trouble getting a room?"

"I've been wondering about that all day." Joseph finished the last of the water, then returned the cup to the saddlebag.

"There probably won't be anything decent left by the time we get there."

Mary's heart clenched with concern. "What will we do when the baby comes?"

He glanced up. "I'm sorry, Mary. I didn't mean to upset you. Don't worry. God will provide something."

"I'm sure you're right." The Lord had sent an angel both to her and to Joseph, and strengthened them when they were rejected by family and friends. Surely He could provide a place for her to give birth to His special Son. He'd probably already prepared the perfect place.

Joseph grinned. "I bet we'll look all over town for a room, and then someone wealthy will take pity on us and invite us in. I can't see God allowing His Son to be born in a public inn."

They continued on their journey down the dusty road, surrounded by others whose ancestors were from Bethlehem. Mary prayed silently, as she'd become accustomed to doing every second she wasn't otherwise occupied. She knew Joseph was doing the same.

"Mary," he whispered, "are you scared?"

"Well ..." She adjusted her position on the donkey. "I've never been to a big city before. I'm nine months pregnant. I've been riding a donkey for five days. And soon I'll give birth to the Son of God." She gave a slight chuckle. "I'm a little tense. What about you?"

Joseph straightened his shoulders. "God'll take care of us. There's nothing to be afraid of."

Mary deeply appreciated her husband's encouragement and his desire to be strong for her.

June gazed out the car window at the slushy hillsides, wondering how much farther they had to go.

"June," Norm whispered, "I'm scared."

She cocked her head at him. "About what?"

He changed lanes to pass a semi moving even more slowly than the cars. "Life is getting to me. It's too complex. And it gets worse at Christmas. If we go to everyone's house, we never have a moment to ourselves. But if we stay home, the whole family gets angry and it takes until Thanksgiving the next year to appease everybody. Then it just starts all over again." He sighed. "What do you think we should do?"

"Maybe we should stop at a restaurant and feed the kids."

Norm slammed a fist against the steering wheel. "You didn't hear a word I said." He shot a glance over his shoulder. "You two shut up and play with the aluminum foil!"

Mary paused at the entrance to the stable, fear gripping her heart. "Joseph, I can't go in there. It's filthy! And it smells. There are bugs and flies." A sharp pain doubled her over. "Quick, Joseph! Get me inside!"

His arm around her waist, Joseph helped Mary walk and then settled her onto a mound of hay. "Just lie down here for a while."

Mary breathed through the pain, as her female relatives had taught her. "I don't mean to be a whiner, but your wealthy someone can come get us any time now."

Joseph squatted beside her, looking helpless. "I'm so sorry." His eyes darted around the stable. "Tell me what I can do."

As the pain eased, Mary did her best to focus. "Build a fire to warm this place up. And find somewhere to lay Jesus when He comes."

Joseph shot to his feet. "I can do that. I'll go get some firewood." He darted out of the stable.

Father God, please be with me now. I know Your Son will be born, and that He'll grow. But … A horrifying thought gripped her. "Joseph!"

He rushed back in. "What's wrong?"

Mary tried to control her breathing. "We know the baby will be fine, but … what if I die in childbirth? Are there any prophecies about that?"

Joseph swallowed hard, then put on a brave face as he knelt beside her. "We have no choice but to trust in God. Please, Mary, be brave … and pray."

What did he think she'd *been* doing?

Her midsection convulsed. "Joseph, I think …" She stopped to catch her breath.

"What, Mary?"

"You should leave."

"I'll never leave you, Mary."

"Joseph, it's time."

"Oh! Okay." He started to go, but turned at the doorway. "I'll be right outside if you need me."

"Go now!"

Joseph practically disappeared into thin air.

"I can't go in there." June sat in the passenger seat, refusing to emerge from the car. "Look at this place. What a dump!" She crossed her arms over her chest. "Merry Christmas, kids. Can you say *botulism*?"

Norm opened his car door. "Hey, be grateful. This is the only joint open between here and Littleton. It is Christmas Eve, you know."

June peered at the neon sign above the entrance, half of its letters unlit. "This isn't a diner. It's a petri dish with a jukebox."

Norm took a deep breath. "All right, everybody, we're leaving." After slamming his door, he restarted the car. "I thought you wanted to feed the kids."

June glanced into the backseat. "Okay, guys, the Jell-O salad is fair game."

Expecting a free-for-all, she was surprised at the silence from her usually rambunctious kids. Looking over her shoulder, she saw them grimacing. "What's wrong?"

"Um …" Billy mumbled.

"We don't really like your Jell-O, Mom."

June gasped. "You do too! I make it every year and you—"

"Nobody likes carrots in their Jell-O," Norm groaned.

June punched him for the thousand and first time.

When she thought about it, she couldn't actually recall seeing either of her children eat her traditional offering. June blew out an exasperated breath. "I can't believe it. Family will turn on you in a heartbeat."

After an uneasy silence, June ventured, "Norman, why don't we—"

"Sell our kids to the next passerby?"

She rolled her eyes. "No. Why don't we tell the kids the Christmas story?"

"What? Where Santa came from?"

"No, the other one. From the Bible."

Norm shrugged. "Okay with me."

June sat up straighter. "All right." She turned to the kids. "Mary and Joseph traveled a long distance while Mary was pregnant."

"How did they travel?" Sally asked.

"I'll bet they took a stage coach," Billy guessed.

"No, honey, they didn't have stage coaches back then." June thought for a moment. "Norm, how did they travel?"

"They were probably carried on those big stretcher things."

"No, they were poor. I think they rode in a chariot or something."

Norm shook his head. "When they got to the town, there was some kind of convention going on, and all the hotels were full. Joseph went from door to door, and nobody had any rooms."

"But one innkeeper felt sorry for them and told them they

could stay in this darling little stable." June grinned, beginning to feel the old Christmas spirit. "They had lots of clean, golden hay to sleep on. There was a gentle cow and the cutest little lamb in the stable with them. And for just that night, the animals could talk."

Norm snorted. "The animals did not talk! You've seen too many cartoons."

June shot a glare at her annoying husband. "Anyway … Mary was sweet, and she had a glow around her face."

"Where does it say that?"

"Look at any manger scene in the world and you can see for yourself."

Norm sighed. "So about that time, it started to snow. And this little drummer boy came into the stable."

"Norman, it has not snowed in Bethlehem since the Ice Age."

"Then why would the little drummer boy go into the stable, huh?"

"Where'd you get a little drummer boy, anyway, Mr. Never Watches Cartoons?"

His jaw dropped. "I can't believe you said that. What would Christmas be without a drummer boy?"

"Quieter?"

Norm's lips tightened to a thin line. "So then one day, the Grinch stole your mother's brain and everybody lived happily ever after!"

Punch one thousand and two.

"So much for lightening the mood."

Spotting a red-and-white-checked building in the distance, with lights glowing in the windows, June pointed. "Hey, what's that?"

"I … I think it's a Bun Boy Restaurant."

"We're saved!"

"Double chili cheeseburgers, here we come! This is gonna be a good Christmas after all." A huge grin split Norm's face. "Come on, kids. Let's sing. 'Jingle bells, Batman smells, Robin laid an egg.'"

Joseph stood in the doorway of the stable, watching Mary sleep. He couldn't take his eyes off the child she'd just delivered, lying beside her.

"I suppose all fathers think their babies are perfect. But this one …"

He knelt beside his new family. "Rest peacefully, my loved ones. After all, what are fathers for if not to protect their families so they can sleep in heavenly peace?"

Life Application

When God does something, He always has a reason—usually several. Why was Jesus born in a stable filled with filth and flies? Because Herod would never look there. Because God wants us to know that He can do anything anywhere. Because Jesus came to be a servant and to teach us to serve too. The list goes on and on.

In the worst possible circumstances, God's plan of redeeming the world was perfectly executed. That's how God often works.

If you're suffering in an unbearable situation, with fears and terrors circling you day and night, don't pray for it all to be fixed. Pray that God would make His presence known. We want things to get better—God wants to be near us and do a perfect work in our lives, to grow us, and to use us to heal and grow others.

God can do great things in your life if you let Him. There's a word for that in Hebrew. *Emmanuel.* It means "God with us."

About the Author

Dave Carl serves as the pastor of children's ministries at Stonebriar Community Church in Frisco, Texas. His wife, Cathy, has patiently put up with him for thirty years. Dave has three kids he loves and one Yorkiepoo he merely endures. He occasionally writes things that are worth reading, and he hopes this piece is one of them.

2

If Not for Grace

by Lori Freeland

The smell of burnt brownies lingered in Blake's too-big-for-one-person kitchen, even after he'd flipped on the fan and shoved open the windows. He glanced at his batter-splattered dress shirt and unrolled his sleeves against a blast of December air. How could he be savvy enough to run financials for an international bank and not be able to master a ninety-nine-cent baking mix?

Chloe's contagious giggle entered the room before she did. Cocooned in a Santa blanket, his niece slid across the slate floor in a pair of reindeer kneesocks, catching herself right before she smacked into the sharp corner of the island.

An emergency-room drama flashed in Blake's head. Complete with a surge of adrenaline. "Slow down, Button."

"Uncle Blake." Chloe wrinkled the nose that had landed her that nickname. "I know what we need."

"Corner guards?" He pressed a hand over his short-circuited heart. Could you bubble wrap an eight-year-old?

Oblivious to his near coronary, she climbed onto the barstool across the counter from him. "We need a wife."

Blake chuckled at the seriousness in her chocolate eyes. "We don't need a wife."

"We do too. No one's going to give a kid to a single guy." She eyed the burnt brownies. "'Specially one who can't cook."

Blake flipped off the fan, wondering again if he was doing the right thing. As much as he loved Chloe, she deserved a family with both a dad and a mom.

"Maybe we should buy brownies instead." Chloe tugged off the part of the blanket she'd used as a hood. Static electricity had a field day with her brown curls.

"Or maybe we should buy a candle that *smells* like brownies." Blake sat on the stool next to hers.

He hadn't realized how empty he'd been until Chloe crashed his shallow existence and proved there was so much more to life than work, eat, sleep, repeat.

Chloe jumped off the stool. "You said the social lady could come anytime this weekend." She stomped a reindeer-covered foot. "If you want her to say you can adopt me, we need a wife. Tonight."

Knowing her little-girl logic might be right slashed at his heart. He knelt in front of her and said softly, "Getting married doesn't work that way." For a second he wished it did. How often did a judge grant custody to a bachelor … under thirty … who wasn't blood related?

"Then what *do* we need?" she asked.

A miracle? It killed him that someone who might not understand how much Chloe meant to him had the right to make such a monumental decision about their lives. "Button—"

"What about that verse from 'Phesians about grace? Grace can save us. God says."

"I don't think that's the kind of saving that Bible verse means—"

"Shh." She squished her eyes closed. "I'm asking God for grace." Her lips moved, but no sound came out.

Chloe's silent prayer squeezed the air from Blake's lungs. He couldn't lose this precious girl who'd hijacked his heart on the worst day of his life—the day he lost his stepsister to the guy he'd begged her not to marry. The guy who cut her off from her family. The guy who ignored three DUIs … and drove his family straight into the back of a truck.

By some miracle, Chloe survived the crash. Her parents and baby brother did not.

Chloe—this niece he'd never known—had come to him like a Christmas-morning gift on the darkest day of July.

"God knows you can't live in this big house alone." Chloe snuggled into his shoulder. "Right?"

"He knows." Blake glanced up. *Please know.* Leashing in his doubt, he leaned back and tapped her chin. "Let's close the windows before you turn into a Chloe-sicle."

While he shut the windows above the sink, Chloe ran to the windows that faced the road. "Blake, look!" She pointed outside.

He joined her and saw a woman in a long coat kneeling next to the front tire of a car parked by their curb. "God listened." Chloe's face lit up brighter than the lights they'd hung outside. "He brought us a wife." She dropped the Santa blanket and darted outside.

"Chloe, wait!" Blake shoved his bare feet into the snowman slippers she'd picked out for him, scooped up her blanket, and took off after her. By the time he made it to the curb, he found her hunched next to the woman. They were staring at a flattening front tire, deep in the middle of a hush-hush conversation.

"Are you good at wife stuff?" Chloe whispered. "Blake can't cook."

Not a conversation. An unauthorized interrogation. "Chloe, stop." Blake wrapped the blanket around her shoulders, pulled her back and up against his chest, and set her socked feet on top of his slippers.

The woman rose and turned. Her coat hung open, revealing a sparkly red cocktail dress. Her hair had been pulled into a fancy knot with soft strands of blonde left free to frame her face. She couldn't be much older than Blake's own age of twenty-eight.

"Blake Butler." He offered his hand over Chloe's shoulder.

"Samantha." She set her hand in his.

He didn't miss her glance at his slippers, the lightning-quick grin she tried to hide, or the way her freezing fingers trembled in his hand before she pulled them away.

Chloe looked at Blake, her face a ball of disappointment. She pulled his head close and spoke into his ear. "Her name's not Grace."

He sighed. Did Chloe really think God would send them a woman named Grace?

"Um …" Samantha nodded toward her car. "I was just—"

Chloe stepped off Blake's feet. "My uncle can fix your tire." She tugged Samantha's hand. "Come inside. I'll make you hot chocolate. With baby marshmallows."

A flicker of uncertainty jumped into Samantha's eyes. "I can probably make it to the service station—"

"It's no problem." Blake smiled. "You got a spare in the trunk?"

"Yes." She dug into a large leather bag, pulled out a set of keys, handed them to Blake, and let Chloe pull her up the walk and into the house.

Changing the tire numbed Blake's fingers, but unlike baking, this was a task he could handle. Good tire on, bad tire thrown in the trunk, he locked the car and headed inside.

"We're waiting for the social lady." Chloe's words filtered from the kitchen. "She decides if Blake can be my dad."

The hope in Chloe's voice hollowed his heart, and he had to pause before he walked into the room.

Judging by the mess on the counter, Chloe had indeed made hot chocolate. She and Samantha sat shoulder to shoulder on the barstools, facing away from him. Samantha's coat hung over a kitchen chair. Her large leather bag lay on the table. And someone had shut the windows.

"All done." Blake rounded the island and returned Samantha's keys.

"Thank you," she said. "I—"

"Samantha isn't married." Chloe's excitement returned in the form of a Disneyland grin. "She's going to a Christmas party. Doesn't she look pretty?"

"Beautiful," Blake said.

"But first she has to finish work."

Work? In a red cocktail dress? A small warning blipped inside Blake's head.

Anxiety darkened the blue in Samantha's eyes. "I think we need to start over." She offered her hand. "I'm Samantha Grace. Department of Social Services."

"She *is* Grace. It's just her *last* name." Chloe's grin inflated.

At the same second, Blake's hope deflated as he ticked off all his daddy failures—ending with Chloe's coatless, shoeless, unsupervised dash outside. Right to a stranger.

"Maybe she knows *our* social lady," Chloe said.

Throat tight, he gently squeezed her shoulder. "Button, Samantha *is* our social worker."

Chloe jumped up and down. "Then you can marry her and everything will be fine."

Blake nearly choked.

"We should talk." Samantha gave him a small smile and pulled a folder out of her bag.

Doing everything he could to keep his face and voice neutral, he tossed Chloe a dish towel. "Why don't you wipe the counter while I show Samantha the Christmas tree?"

On the way to the den, his feet did a death-row shuffle.

Samantha sat in the wing chair by the tree. He perched on the edge of the sofa across from her, wondering if there was any way they really could start over.

"You have a unique situation, Mr. Butler." She clutched the file.

Unique. That didn't sound good.

"I've been on your side ever since I read your petition. But when Chloe came running out …"

He winced. "You've changed your mind."

She set down the file. "When I was thirteen, my dad died. My mom had left us years before. A distant cousin took me in." Her gaze found Blake's. "The way you are with Chloe …" She paused. "Kind. Caring. Adam was like that with me. Chloe obviously loves you."

"But?" He steeled himself for whatever words she'd use to deem him unfit father material.

"No buts. You passed. I knew the second Chloe started interviewing me to be your wife." She chuckled.

A vice released his lungs. "I passed?"

"Told ya." Chloe flew into the den and into his arms. "God sent us Grace."

"You're right," he whispered into her ear. "God sent us *His* grace."

Standing, Samantha touched Chloe's curls. "Merry Christmas, Mr. Butler."

"Thank you," he mouthed over Chloe's head, then gazed upward. *And thank You.*

Life Application

While God doesn't always send a person to answer our every prayer, He did send His Son with a different type of grace—a saving grace that is the real meaning behind Christmas. Ephesians 2:8 says, "It is by grace you have been saved, through faith—and this is not from yourselves, it is the gift of God."

While Chloe gave this verse an eight-year-old spin, the truth of God's promise remains. God looks at a much bigger picture than we do. The Lord of all creation longs for us to choose Him as our Father in a much bigger way than Chloe chose Blake to be her dad. He wants us for eternity.

About the Author

Lori Freeland is a writing teacher and coach for the North Texas Christian Writers and a contributor to Crosswalk.com and Believe.com. She's addicted to flavored coffee and imaginary people. When she's not writing inspirational articles, she's working on several young-adult novels. Visit her website, lafreeland.com, or look for L. A. Freeland on Facebook.

3

The Christmas Child of 1864

by Lena Nelson Dooley

Each hesitant footstep sounded a hollow drumbeat in the nearly empty house. Marion wandered from room to room, mourning more than the loss of her parents. Yes, this Christmas would be lonely without Mother and Father, but she'd had almost a year to get used to them being gone. Last winter, when influenza raged through the countryside, robbing numerous families of members, Marion questioned why God allowed her to live while He took her lovely mother. Marion couldn't be sorry that her father had also succumbed to the dreaded disease. Ever since he came home from the fighting without either of his legs, he had been only a shell of the man who marched valiantly to the war, confident that the South would quickly win.

How long could a war last? It had been three agonizing years. Years that had stolen more than the young manhood of the South. They had slowly leeched the wealth as well. That was what Marion mourned most this clear, sunny, cold

December day. The loss of so many of the family's prized possessions.

As she entered the music room, her gaze flew to the corner where the ebony piano had reigned as the monarch. How she missed sitting on the stool and running her fingers up and down the ivory keys, releasing the notes held captive there—music that lilted through the air and comforted her, whatever her distress. But the piano had been the first piece of furniture to go, and for such a small sum. Mother had been distressed, but the meager funds carried them through almost a month while Father fought the demons of pain and the other agonies he'd brought home with him.

Other treasured heirlooms had followed the piano: the rosewood desk her grandfather built for her grandmother as a wedding present, the elegant sideboard with the stained-glass doors, the china her great-grandparents brought from England as newlyweds. As the third son of a nobleman, her great-grandfather had left his ancestral home to make a life in America. And he had done well. This plantation was a tribute to his determination to be his own man. It had sustained a growing family … and a growing number of slaves.

What a pity Father had gone to war. He didn't believe in slavery, but he did believe in something he called "state's rights." Soon after he and Mother had married, they freed all their slaves, even educated them. Because of this, most of the Negroes had stayed on, and the plantation continued to prosper.

When Father went off to war, many of the freed slaves moved to the North, leaving Mother without enough people to help run the plantation. Every year had become harder.

With Father returning in such bad shape, Mother lost heart. She spent all her time trying to make him comfortable and attempting to restore his self-confidence.

Now Marion had to run the plantation without them. With the help of Daisy and Joshua, the two remaining Negroes, she had done the best she could.

"Miss Marion?" Daisy's smooth molasses voice called from the parlor. "Where are you?"

Marion retraced her steps to the warmest room in the house, the only one where they kept a fire burning in the daytime. "What is it?" She looked across the large space.

Daisy sat before the blazing fire, peeling wrinkled sweet potatoes. The parlor had been stripped of all but a few pieces of furniture. Three chairs sat in front of the fireplace, with a small round table beside one of them. So little in such a large room that had once been crowded.

"I think someone's comin' up from the road."

Marion looked out one of the front windows, peeking from behind the drapes, kept closed against the cold. She didn't see anything, but she detected the faint sound of hoofbeats on the packed dirt of the drive. "Who could it be? I hope it's not Union soldiers."

"Lawsy, Miss Marion, surely not." Fear caused Daisy to revert to her old way of speaking. She quickly gathered up the potatoes she was working on and scurried to the cookhouse, no doubt to look for Joshua.

A ramshackle wagon drawn by two scrawny mules came

into Marion's view. It was driven by one of the squatters who had settled on a burned-out and abandoned plantation a few miles away. He drove slowly, looking at a lump in the back of the wagon as much as he looked at the road ahead. Marion wondered what the pile of quilts covered.

The man carefully stopped the wagon. He stared at the house for a long moment before climbing down and heading for the front door.

Marion breathed a sigh of relief when Joshua answered the visitor's timid summons. She scanned the surroundings for signs of enemy soldiers.

"Miss Marion." Joshua stood at the door to the parlor. "This man and his wife need help."

"Are you sure it's not a trap?"

"I don't think so. His wife is about to have a baby, and he doesn't know what to do."

Marion trembled. She had been sixteen when her father went off to war. In the three years since, she'd learned how to take care of the plantation … what was left of it. But she didn't know anything about childbirth.

"How can we help her?"

"Daisy was a right good midwife in her day. She could help if it's all right with you, Miss Marion."

How could she turn them away? There wasn't anyone else close by who could help them. Besides, this was Christmas Eve. Maybe having a baby born here would make it seem more festive.

"Help the man bring her in. I'll go get Daisy."

By the time Marion returned to the house with Daisy, the men had settled the poor woman on a pallet in front of the fireplace. The husband crouched beside her, holding her hand as she moaned and writhed.

When the two women entered the parlor, he stood, turning toward them with an expression of relief. "I'll help your man put the horse and wagon away." The men eagerly left the room.

While Marion watched, Daisy examined the pregnant woman and made her pallet more comfortable.

The men reentered the house. Marion heard their muffled voices in the hall.

Daisy sent Marion to the cookhouse to set water on to boil. She also asked her to get some of the older linens and tear them into strips to prepare for the birth.

As Marion passed the large entrance hall, she saw the agitated husband pacing the floor. Joshua was trying to soothe him. She stood at the linen closet, listening to their conversation.

"You don't seem like an excited new father to me." Joshua sounded almost condemning, which wasn't typical of the gentle man.

"How can I be excited? It's not my baby." The man spat out the words as if he couldn't stand their bitter taste.

"You said she's your wife."

"That she is."

"Was she carrying another man's child when you married?" Joshua's tone had softened.

"No." The man paused. "Some soldiers came by right after we built our shanty. I couldn't tell which side they were on.

Maybe they were renegades. They took everything they could load onto their horses, and then they …"

"And you think the child is from that?"

"My wife hasn't been the same since it happened. She hasn't wanted to be touched. Even by me. I've tried to understand. I wanted to be gentle with her, so I didn't push her before she was ready. Then she told me she was with child."

Marion's heart broke for the man … and for the woman who labored in the parlor. She peeked around the door and saw Joshua gently place his large hand on the man's shoulder.

"But you were together as man and wife before it happened. It could be your child."

"No. She had her … womanly time before they came, and we never …"

Joshua bowed his grizzled head and murmured too low for Marion to hear, but she knew he was praying with the man. They stayed that way for a long time, and she didn't want to interrupt.

She took her sewing basket off the shelf of the linen closet. With her scissors, she cut a sheet into strips, all the while murmuring a prayer for the couple.

"Are you a God-fearing man?" Joshua's question startled Marion.

"Yes, sir, I am."

"I'm sure Joseph must have felt the way you do when Mary first told him about carrying the Christ child. But he was the father the boy needed. And this child needs you for his father."

The man nodded, tears rimming his eyes.

A tiny cry pealed from the parlor, followed by Daisy's exclamation, "It's a boy!"

As she rushed to take the cloths to the mother and the infant, Marion thought, *This truly is a special Christmas.*

Life Application

Our lives take many unexpected twists and turns. Wars destroy family unity. Relationships sour and we don't know how to heal them. Economic downturns take away our sense of security. Pink slips wave in the wind as jobs disappear. Nothing in this world is certain.

As Christians, we should look to the Lord whenever we find ourselves in difficult circumstances. When things happen in my life that I don't understand, I often wonder how God can work those things together for good, as Romans 8:28 promises. But somehow He does. Sometimes a situation looks so bleak I can't imagine how God could possibly use it for anything positive. But He always comes through. And I know He always will.

About the Author

Lena Nelson Dooley is an award-winning, multi-published author who loves to mentor the writers God brings to her. She's been married to the love of her life for more than fifty years. They live in Texas. Lena speaks at retreats, conferences, and writers' meetings. Her website is lenanelsondooley.com. On her blog (lenanelsondooley.blogspot.com), she introduces new releases of other authors to readers around the world.

4

Camouflaged Christmas

by Beverly Nault

Brooke surveyed the sparse nursery, grateful that the three-month-old nestled on her shoulder had finally fallen asleep. In their holiday haste, the movers had left her and Jason's rented duplex a jumbled chaos of cartons and furniture. She sighed at the mess, determined to be a good army wife and bear up under the strain of new motherhood.

Her husband's deployment announcement had not been unexpected. But between raging postpartum hormones, lack of sleep, and the challenge of relocating to a new town to be near her parents, Brooke had to constantly fight her broiling emotions.

"Where do you want this?" Jason's green eyes shone as he hefted a carton marked "Christmas."

"Just set it on the screened-in porch." Biting her tongue to keep from adding, *as if there's anything worth celebrating*, Brooke shifted Max to her other arm, careful not to wake him.

She'd promised herself to stop bothering Jason with her anxieties. Every time she peppered him with questions about how long he'd be gone, he repeated, "Three to six months. That's not so bad." But half a year felt like half a lifetime, especially when she thought of how much he would miss of his only child's early development.

Jason set down the box. "We'll video chat. And I'll call whenever I can, babe."

His reassurances didn't help, but she snuggled into his comforting embrace, knowing he would soon be too far away to hold her. She was grateful that he'd been given permission to stay behind because of complications with her pregnancy and Max's early birth. But he needed to join his unit as soon as possible.

"We'll miss you." Her remark wasn't as light as she'd hoped, but Jason smiled anyway.

Their last few days passed in a flurry and before she knew it, Brooke was waving good-bye as Jason's taxi whisked him away. She'd tucked inside his duffle bag a small gift that he could open on Christmas Day.

Tears stinging her eyes, she put her overnight suitcase in the car beside Max, who was gurgling in his infant seat. Her parents' address entered into the GPS, she pulled away to drive the unfamiliar streets. Recently retired, they'd moved to Florida several months before Max was born, downsizing to a fifty-five-plus community. Days later, Jason had received the overseas orders that rocked Brooke's world.

The Bluetooth tone pinged, and Brooke answered.

"Honey, your aunt—" The bad cell connection stole every

other word. But Brooke detected an anxious tone in her mother's voice that told her something was wrong. "… very critical … leaving …"

"W-what?" Brooke stammered. "Mom, I can barely hear you."

"Aunt Christine … stroke. We're … way to the airport. I'm so sorry …"

"When will you be back?"

The connection died. Brooke braked for a red light. "I can't believe I'm going to be alone for Christmas!" She wiped at a tear and considered heading for the airport herself. But she didn't cherish traveling with an infant again. The flight out here had shattered her nerves—and those of everyone else on board.

A text pinged in and she glanced down.

We'll try to be back by Christmas. Go ahead to the house. I made a roast last night. There's still some left in the fridge. The spare key is with our neighbor, Penny. Make yourself at home. Love, Mom.

Brooke thought of the empty refrigerator in the duplex. Leftover roast sounded great about now.

The radio blared yet another cheerful holiday carol. Brooke switched the annoying thing off.

No husband, no family, no friends. And in this wretchedly sunshiny state, not even any snow. By the time she pulled into her parents' neighborhood, she was weeping. She took a few minutes to compose herself before fumbling to get Max out of the car and carrying him to the next-door neighbor's house.

When the door opened to her knock, a tiny bell in a small

wreath tinkled. Brooke found herself looking down upon a head of close-cropped, snow-white hair over stooped shoulders.

"Yes?"

"Are you Penny? I'm Brooke Thompson." Impatient, she spoke too quickly. Forcing herself to slow down, she added, "My parents said you had a key to their house."

A moment of confusion passed, and a crooked finger poked up at her. "Oh, yes. Bonnie and Dick's girl."

"Yes, ma'am. Bonnie and *Rick*." The sun pounded down, and Max fussed a complaint. "If I could just get the key."

"Hold on."

Penny disappeared inside, and Brooke moved to some shade behind an abundant bougainvillea, worried Max's delicate skin would burn.

"Here you are." Penny joined her again. "I hope your aunt is all right."

"Thanks," Brooke mumbled, then rushed to get the key in the lock before her baby baked like a stuffed turkey in the Florida heat.

"Merry Christmas," Penny called from her front stoop.

"You too." Brooke shut the door just before her waterworks erupted again. *Merry Christmas indeed.*

Brooke spent the evening putting ornaments on a small artificial tree while Max contently sucked on his newly discovered toes. When she finished, she tucked the baby into a travel crib in the guest room.

As she emerged, she noticed flashing lights outside. Curious, she opened the front door and saw a gurney being wheeled from the porch next door toward an ambulance waiting at the curb.

Brooke hurried out to Penny, who was being pushed by one paramedic and watched over by another.

"Are you all right?" Brooke touched the woman's thin shoulder.

Penny pulled the oxygen mask off her face. "Bad ticker," came the muffled reply.

The EMT tried to replace the mask, which Penny fought. "We really need to get you moving, ma'am."

"Just give me a minute, please." Her firm tone left no room for argument.

Penny grasped Brooke's hand with surprising strength. "Honey, I want you to do me a favor. There's an envelope in my room. By my bed. Please go get it and …" Penny's breath labored, and the medic replaced the mask, cutting short the rest of her request.

"We're taking her to County Hospital," the EMT told Brooke. "You can check on her there."

After the ambulance drove off, Brooke tried Penny's front door and found it locked—the paramedics must have seen to that. How was she supposed to get into the house for the mystery envelope? And what was she was supposed to do with it if she found it?

The next morning, she called her parents. They had made the trip safely, but her aunt was still critical, so they'd have to stay a few extra days.

When Brooke told her mother about Penny and the envelope, she said, "We keep her spare key on the back of the cupboard door next to the pantry."

With Max dozing in his carrier, Brooke let herself inside Penny's cottage. In the bedroom she found a large envelope on a bedside table, with "Lara Adele Lewis" and an address printed in shaky handwriting.

Back in her parents' kitchen, Brooke dialed the hospital, and the receptionist connected her.

"Did you open it?" Penny's voice brightened when Brooke mentioned her success.

"I didn't want to pry."

"It's all right."

Inside the envelope, Brooke found a grainy black-and-white photo of a woman in a long skirt, her hair in a bun sprigged with wildflowers, her midsection bulging with new life. She stood beside a man in a suit with a high, starched collar.

"Those are my grandparents," Penny purred. "The picture was taken just before my grandfather left for the war. She never saw him again."

A lump formed in Brooke's throat, preventing her from speaking.

"I promised my granddaughter I'd send it to her." Penny paused for a shallow breath. "Now that she's expecting, she's interested in our family tree."

Brooke swallowed back a sob. "Do you want me to mail the picture for you?"

"If you wouldn't mind. I'm not sure how long I'll be in here."

"I'll do it right away." Any excuse to hang up and end this uncomfortable conversation.

"Your mom told me about your husband leaving." Penny's tone was soft. "I'll bet you could use a friend. Especially as you prepare to celebrate the Savior's birth."

Her offer softened Brooke's stubborn resolve.

"My own son was in Vietnam." Penny choked back a sob. "When you talk to your husband next, please thank him for his service to our freedom."

Penny's voice was so quiet, Brooke could barely hear her. "I will. Thank you. I wish I could visit you, but with the baby—"

"Maybe instead you could visit my Lara. She's on bed rest due to some complications with her pregnancy. She could use a friend her age. She lives down the freeway a bit. Her address is on the envelope."

"I'd be happy to visit her." And she could take the picture to her in person.

Brooke took a deep breath, compelled to ask a question even though the answer might not be what she wanted to hear. "Your son. Do you mind if I ask …"

"Lara's dad came back in one piece. He lives in Georgia now."

A rush of relief filled Brooke's heart. "I'm so glad. I should let you rest now. Merry Christmas, Penny."

"Merry Christmas to you, too, dear."

Gazing at Max, Brooke knew that even though Jason was absent, he was where he was supposed to be, and so was she. She could almost feel her husband's love from thousands of miles away. She uttered a quick prayer of gratitude for the reminder that she could trust God to take care of her.

She smiled and picked up the baby, settled in front of the computer, then logged into Skype so they could wish their warrior the merriest Christmas ever.

Life Application

Brooke focused on her own expectations and disappointments, failing to appreciate her husband's sacrifice until Penny needed her. When God used Brooke in her unique place, the scales of selfishness fell from her eyes and she could finally see what He had in store for her and how she could serve Him.

In 1 Peter, we are reminded to use the abilities God has gifted us with to serve one another and that our obedience brings Him glory. No matter where He places us, He strengthens us to serve Him.

"Each one, as a good manager of God's different gifts, must use for the good of others the special gift he has received from God … so that in all things praise may be given to God through Jesus Christ, to whom belong glory and power forever and ever" (1 Peter 4:10–11 GNT).

While everyone else celebrates the holidays with families and friends, our soldiers, health-care workers, paramedics, police, and firefighters must report for duty. What can you do this season to cheer a lonely heart?

About the Author

Beverly Nault writes from Southern California. Her warrior husband, Gary, flew A-10s in the United States Air Force and served in Operation Desert Storm while she prayed for him and cared for Lindsay and Evan until Daddy came home. This story is dedicated to all American military families.

5

The Christmas Star

by Charles Lober

After tonight, Paige said to herself, *I will be a celebrity*. She viewed her image in the dressing-room mirror. With trembling hands, she fastened the leather belt around her white tunic. Running a comb through her curly auburn hair, she smiled at the sight of her freckled face.

She could just see the review in tomorrow's *New York Times*: "There was more than one new 'star of Bethlehem' last night. The lead actress, Paige Humphries, was magnificent in the role of Mary, exhibiting a talent rarely seen on Broadway. At the tender age of twenty-eight, she has a bright future ahead of her."

Paige lifted the hem of her tunic and stepped into the leather sandals. She descended the stairs and arrived backstage just in time for her warm-up exercises. After taking a deep breath of the cold, musty air, she slowly recited, "The Christmas cake with colored candles was cut by Clara Claus." She repeated it quickly three times without faltering. Then she gently rolled her shoulders back and forth, releasing the tension in her muscles. Goose bumps rose on her arms as the roar of the huge crowd pounded in her ears. Act Two had just ended.

Paige waited for the curtain to fall before taking her position at stage right. A crew member had placed the manger—her main prop—at center stage. The monologue she was about to deliver was the chance she had been waiting for since she was a little girl. Her heart began to race and she could feel the blood pulsing through her veins. She thought the intermission would never end. Finally, the director gave Paige a thumbs-up, signaling one minute before the final act.

As the curtain rose, a hush fell over the room. From the stage canopy, one light began to shine brighter and brighter, forming a circle on the stage floor. Paige's moment had arrived!

She stepped into the circle and was instantly transformed—like a butterfly emerging from its chrysalis. Her nervousness subsided, and in its place surged a wave of confidence, bold and exciting. Looking up at the light, she began her first line.

"Oh, star of Bethlehem, how wondrous you are. Out of all the stars in the heavens, God chose you to herald His wondrous gift." She put on her biggest smile. "At your sight, the wise men rejoiced."

The circle moved slowly in the direction of the manger. Paige glided across the stage, careful to stay within the star's orb. When she reached the foot of the manger, bathed in a soft blue radiance, she said, "By your guiding light, the wise men reached their destination." She knelt and bowed her head.

"And under your watchful gaze, they stood in the presence of the Christ child, worshipping Him."

Paige faced the audience. "God loves each and every one of you. Enough to offer you the gift of His only Son."

Extending her arms high above her head, she exclaimed, "He is the source of true joy." Her voice echoed throughout the auditorium.

She lowered her arms to waist high. "He is the light who guides our every step."

She wrapped her arms around herself and said in a stage whisper, "He is the companion who is always with you. Jesus' last words before He left this world were 'And surely I am with you always, to the very end of the age.'"

Paige clasped her hands over her chest. "So open the door of your heart and follow *your* star." As the lights went down, she lowered her head.

The audience stood and cheered. Paige took one bow, then another. As she reached down to scoop up the bouquets of flowers thrown at her feet, she heard a loud clanging noise. *Don't mess up my big moment.* But the sound drowned out the roar of the crowd.

Paige clapped her hands over her ears, glared at the old water heater in the corner of her basement, and sighed. "Dad really needs to fix that awful thing," she muttered.

When she returned her attention to the "stage," the star of Bethlehem was just a bare bulb hanging from the ceiling, the manger an empty wooden crate. There was no cheering audience, no flowers—just a twelve-year-old girl alone with her dreams. As loneliness engulfed her, Paige's legs trembled and tears welled up in her eyes.

Why do Mom and Dad leave me at home so often? Other kids' parents took them shopping. Or to the movies. Or on vacations. *At least they could take me to work with them.*

A car door squeaked open outside, then slammed shut. High-heeled shoes clicked on the sidewalk. Keys jangled as the front door swung open.

"Paige," her mother hollered. "Are you in the cellar again?"

"Yes, ma'am."

Mom appeared at the top of the stairs. "Honey, I've told you not to go down there when I'm gone. Hurry up now and wash your hands. I'm making your favorite: macaroni and cheese."

Paige flung the bed sheet off her shoulders and tossed it onto the wooden crate. She neatly folded the script she had borrowed from her parents' room, glad that she had listened to Mom rehearse for the church play. Some words were hard for her to pronounce, but she had practiced saying the lines whenever she got the chance. She tucked the paper into her shirt pocket.

She headed toward the stairs, then stopped when the last line of the play came back to her mind.

And surely I am with you always.

Paige's heart leapt. Even when no one else was around, she was never really alone. God had promised to be with her, to guide her every step and to calm her every fear.

"Paige!" Mom called again.

"Coming!" She pivoted and bowed one last time, throwing

a farewell kiss to her imaginary audience. Then she bounded up the steps.

Life Application

A dear friend of mine told me that when she was a child, she sometimes had to stay home alone. To pass the time and fend off loneliness, she liked to go to the basement—even though it was somewhat dark and scary—and pretend to be in a play. The light shining in through the window made an oval shape on the basement floor. She would stand in the "spotlight" and act out scenes from her favorite stories. Her performances were always met with standing ovations.

When I reflect on God's gift of His only Son, I want to give Him a standing ovation. In one daring move prompted by love, God set in motion His plan for bringing us back into fellowship with Him. Jesus declared Himself to be the Light of the World and promised that those who follow Him will not walk in darkness, but will have the Light of life (John 8:12).

With Christ in our lives, we are never alone. He will guide our every step if we allow Him to.

About the Author

Charles Lober is the author of The Christmas Club trilogy: *The Riverside Club, The Last Chance Friends' Club,* and *The Club Homecoming*. You can read more of Paige's story in *The Riverside Club.* Charles lives with his wife, Sandra, and their daughter, Nicole Alejandra, in Birmingham, Alabama.

6

Jackson's Daughter

by Nancy Arant Williams

Jane didn't want to open her eyes. She didn't even want to get out of bed, even though tomorrow was Christmas, her favorite time of the year.

With a sigh, she threw off the covers, migrated to the kitchen, and turned on the coffee maker. In the shower, she spotted a gray hair that hadn't been there yesterday. Who got gray hair in their thirties? Apparently she did.

Through the bathroom window she winced at the brilliant sunshine. A sullen, cloudy sky would have been more appropriate.

How will I ever get through this day?

She forced down a piece of toast, chasing it with sips of coffee, but the taste was off. Everything seemed off. Nothing looked the same as it did yesterday morning, when her world fell apart.

Today she had to pick out her father's casket.

On the way to the mortuary, she stopped to fill her car with gas. Christmas carols played through a loudspeaker from inside the building. People smiled and wished each other Merry Christmas. Why didn't the world stop revolving and stand still when her life crashed to a screeching halt? It was like a cruel joke to have to bury someone you loved at Christmas.

At the mortuary, a skinny man in his sixties shook her hand and told her how sorry he was for her loss. Why couldn't funeral directors be fat and jolly and wear pastels? It would help so much if they were exactly the opposite of what you'd expect.

After taking down the details of her father's life, from which he would later compose an obituary, he led her to the casket room. The walls were painted peach, and the soft lights gave a rosy glow to the caskets.

"Feel free to browse. I'll be back in a few minutes."

Jane felt a headache gnawing at the base of her neck. She rolled her head and massaged her shoulders with her fingers.

How does someone go about picking a casket? Just like choosing a car, she supposed, as awful as that sounded. Her dad's take on the subject of purchasing anything: compare prices, get the best value for the dollar, and buy as much quality as you could afford. He'd been a salesman by trade, so he had figured it all out.

Jane was only six years old when her mom died. Ever since, her world had revolved around Dad. She never expected him to die in a car accident, especially at just fifty-six years old.

The only clear memory she had of her mother was of hair ribbons. Her hands always seemed to be full of them, tying them around Jane's pigtails. *Funny how I can see her hands but never her face.*

Oh, Dad, will your face fade from my memory too?

With tears clouding her vision, she began turning over price tags on caskets. The man would be back shortly, expecting an answer.

One really ugly coffin caught her eye. *I'd want to live forever if that was my casket.*

When the emergency-room doctor told her that her father was dead, she kept repeating, "No, he's not. You're wrong. My dad will never die."

But there he was, lying on a gurney in that cold, white hospital room, looking like a stranger. Without his trademark Chiefs baseball cap, his head looked naked. She hadn't even noticed how gray his hair had turned over the years.

Jane had searched his face for a long time to make sure it was really him. She didn't want to see it, but the small scar on his chin was proof of his identity.

She had taken the hand she'd held so often and kissed it. It was frighteningly cool.

The mortuary man appeared in the doorway. "Do you have any questions?"

"Only one."

"Yes?"

She worked up a smile reminiscent of her father's notorious wry wit. "The tag on that jazzy oak number says it has a one-hundred-year warranty against insects, mold and mildew, water damage, and deterioration. Would you dig it up at the end of one hundred years and stand behind that promise?"

He blinked at her as if she were insane. Maybe she was.

He rubbed his left temple. "That was a joke, right?"

"No. My dad always wanted to make sure he was getting his money's worth."

"Well …" He cleared his throat. "After one hundred years, none of us will be around to see if the casket is intact. If I were still here, I would be happy to …"

"No, you wouldn't."

He spread his hands wide in defeat. "What do you want me to say?"

"I just want you to be honest."

"Okay." He shrugged. "What you see is what you get."

"Thank you."

"So, have you made a decision?"

"I think I want the white pine one. Dad was a master carpenter, and pine was his favorite wood."

"An excellent choice."

She looked him in the eye. "Do you patronize all of your customers?"

He frowned. "I'm sorry, but I don't know what you're getting at."

"You need to be real," she said. "People don't want platitudes. They appreciate simple honesty and kindness."

"I apologize. I will try to be more … real."

"Good enough."

He set the credit-card slip in front of her, and she signed it.

Jane felt better as she strode to her car, knowing her father would've been pleased with the transaction. And though she would never stop missing him, she knew she could rest, knowing he was in heaven, telling jokes and making people smile just as he always had. She could practically see it now.

Perhaps with the new year swiftly approaching, it wasn't the end after all, but a brand-new beginning.

Life Application

Are you struggling with feelings of loss and grief in this season of joy? Does it seem as if you'll never recover? You can take comfort in knowing that one of the names of God is Jehovah Shama, the God who is ever present. He is right there with you at all times, promising never to leave you alone. He is your comforter, so ask Him to wrap you in His loving embrace. Ask Him to help you see things through heaven's eyes and give you His perspective.

Psalm 40:1–3 tells us, "I waited patiently for the Lord; and He inclined to me and heard my cry. He brought me up out of the pit of destruction, out of the miry clay, and He set my feet upon a rock making my footsteps firm. He put a new song in my mouth, a song of praise to our God" (NASB).

God is there for you, ready to provide whatever you need. So seek Him today.

About the Author

Nancy Arant Williams is a multi-published author and book editor. She and her husband live in the heart of the beautiful wooded Missouri Ozarks, where they welcome guests to exit the rat race and rest at The Nestle Down Inn Bed & Breakfast. Her greatest desire is for people to realize how deeply God loves them. Check out her websites: nancyarantwilliams.com and nestledowninn.com.

7

The Balsam Walk

by Joanne Bischof

There are a few things only poor kids do. Wear decades-old hand-me-downs. Add water to a can of SpaghettiOs. And wait until nearly dusk on Christmas Eve to get a tree. Which is why Becca Fletcher was towing a small sled along the edge of the curvy mountain highway, wearing a skirt that was once her great-aunt's, and dreaming of a really cheesy slice of pizza. With her sights on Harmony Farms, the local feed store that sold Christmas trees, she was glad the log building was only two miles from home.

When the store came into view, decorated in twinkly lights and a dusting of fresh snow, Becca slowed. A young man stood by the side of the road. Maybe a bit older than her seventeen, with the golden skin and dark eyes of a Pacific Islander. He wore jeans, black combat boots, and a hooded jacket. Marker in hand, he scribbled something on a piece of cardboard, then set the sign beside a pile of spindly Christmas trees.

Though Becca hadn't seen him in years, she recognized Riley Kane. When they were kids, they'd made dried-pasta necklaces and cotton-ball sheep together in Sunday school. Rumor had it his dad had hit the road long ago and not looked back. Riley's name had recently made it onto the prayer chain her mom was part of—something about him nearly having gone to juvenile hall.

And now she was alone with him on the side of the road. Terrific.

When he noticed her staring at him, his gaze narrowed. She forced herself to take steps forward. Everyone knew the feed store put leftover trees by the highway on Christmas Eve. So why was he eying her like she'd come to rob the place?

Wondering if he recognized her, she offered a weak smile. Unsettled by his silent scrutiny, she looked to the heap at his feet. The trees weren't in the greatest shape, but she wasn't picky. Her younger brothers and sisters would be thrilled with anything.

In the midst of the pile of castoffs, she spotted a large, full tree. Becca pulled her sled over and touched a branch. Its needles were soft. She checked the tag—a six-foot balsam from Washington. Bound snug in netting, it smelled heavenly.

"Is this one free?" she asked, peeking back at him.

He nodded.

She began to tug the beauty onto her sled. Good grief, the thing was heavy.

Riley moved in beside her. "Let me help you with that."

"Thank you."

He heaved the tree onto the sled, then straightened and tugged off his black beanie. He pushed dark, shaggy hair off to the side before replacing his hood. He eyed her for a moment, his gaze sliding down to the boots she'd just gotten at the thrift store. Becca fought the urge to shimmy her feet farther under her skirt.

She grabbed the rope and thanked him again. He pulled an iPod from his pocket, tucked a pair of earbuds into place, then hit a button.

Becca tugged on the sled. Her shoes slipped in the snow. She tugged again. And slipped again. Tug. Slip. She pulled harder, then nearly fell.

Riley reached out, then hesitated. "Want help with that?" Snowflakes fell around them. Several dusted the top of his black hood.

"I'll just get one of the smaller trees," she said.

He scrunched his nose. "No need. I can help you. I'm off now anyway."

After she thanked him, he walked back to the store, carried a few sacks of feed inside, then quickly locked up. He unplugged the Christmas lights and started back toward the highway. At her side once again, he gently took the rope from her and tugged the sled into motion.

"I'm Riley."

"Rebecca."

They clomped on in silence, him pulling the heavy load.

"Are you sure you don't mind?" she asked.

"Not at all." He gave her a small smile, though it seemed

forced. When the silence continued a little longer, he kicked at a clump of snow. “I haven’t seen you around church lately.”

So he did remember her. “We’ve been attending the Baptist church. It’s close enough to walk to.”

“Gotcha.”

The coming sunset blasted a pale pink over the mountain peaks. A car sped by, throwing up icy gravel.

“How far to your house?”

“About a mile from here. Want me to pull for a while?”

He tossed his head, shifting his bangs out of his eyes. “You tried that already, remember?”

The dry way he said it made her smile.

As if that emboldened him, he talked on a little more. When the sled wedged on a root sticking out of the snow, he had to stop and adjust the runners. “Do you always get your trees at Harmony Farms?” he asked as they started on again.

“Every time. A neighbor picked one up for us last year.”

“On Christmas Eve?”

She nodded, feeling a little embarrassed to confess that.

Riley’s brow pinched. “A guy with gray hair driving an old pickup truck?”

“That’s right!” Becca rubbed her chilled hands together. “I’m amazed you remember.”

“He said it was for a family with a bunch of kids, so Mrs. Lawrence threw in a couple of poinsettias.”

She smiled at the memory of those potted plants that had brought so much color and cheer to their home.

As they walked on, he asked why he had never seen her

at school. He seemed amused by her "homeschooled" declaration.

"Do you like that?"

"It has its advantages. I get to do schoolwork in my pj's and I'm always done by lunch."

"I'm a little jealous." He chuckled.

Their shoes crunched in the snow, and she felt him glance at her more than once. When his gaze was on the path ahead, she stole a peek of her own. He was a good-looking guy, but her mom had taught her not to let physical appearance distract from the qualities that mattered most: kindness, honesty, faith.

Becca was about to glance at him again when he asked about her family.

By the time they dipped into the valley, where small cabins and trailers speckled the snowy woods, she'd told him she had five siblings, her father was a truck driver for a local dairy, and though he was gone a lot, he was pretty much her hero.

She nearly said more about her father when she remembered the rumors of Riley's dad. Instead, she gently asked about his family.

"My mom and I lived here for a while after my dad left. We've moved around a lot since then, mostly in Orange County. But I came back here after graduation."

"And your dad?"

Riley panted a bit. "He's in Hawaii. That's where he's from. He's a professional surfer … has sponsors and everything. He travels all over the world." He drew a heavy breath. "I get postcards from time to time." He looked away.

Not knowing what to say about that, she changed the subject. "Have you worked at the feed store long?"

His dark eyes gazed at her for so long, she was worried he might bump into a tree. "A couple of years." He looked back to the path ahead. "I like working there, and it covers the rent."

Becca spotted her family's silver Airstream trailer nestled beneath snowy pines, a wreath hanging from the narrow metal door. "Thanks for the help." She spoke the words slowly, not quite ready to say good-bye. "I really appreciate it."

He tugged the sled to a stop. "I can set the tree up for you … if you want." One side of his mouth lifted. "I do lots of deliveries, so tree installation is kind of a specialty of mine."

"Tree installation?"

"It's a real thing."

Becca nearly laughed. But she detected a bit of yearning in his expression—as if he longed for something he hadn't had in a while: family.

She motioned toward the trailer. "Come on in, then. Would you like a cup of cider? We just have the powdered kind. But my sisters and I made sugar cookies today."

"I like cider and cookies." His mouth quirked.

Her cheeks warm, for more reasons than one, Becca opened the door and Riley lugged the tree inside. Shrieks filled the air as her brothers and sisters rushed him. He smiled as he wrestled the fragrant balsam to an upright position.

Riley pulled a utility knife from his pocket. After a few slices, the bindings fell to the ground and green branches burst free. The trailer all but shook with excitement. Shouts and whoops sounded over the radio playing Christmas music.

The trailer filled with the fresh scent of balsam as Becca watched Riley work. Suddenly, she didn't mind being poor. If her circumstances were different, she never would've been in that tree lot on Christmas Eve. She wouldn't have taken that walk home with Riley. Perhaps the presents her mom tucked under the tree would be bigger—but there was no way any smiles could be any brighter.

Life Application

We all touch other people's lives in different ways. Sometimes a little help or friendship can make a big difference. We never know whom we may bump into or how God may use us to bless or encourage another person.

"As each has received a gift, use it to serve one another, as good stewards of God's varied grace: whoever speaks, as one who speaks oracles of God; whoever serves, as one who serves by the strength that God supplies—in order that in everything God may be glorified through Jesus Christ. To him belong glory and dominion forever and ever. Amen" (1 Peter 4:10–11 ESV).

In what ways can you be a blessing in an unexpected way this holiday season?

About the Author

Joanne Bischof, Christy Award finalist and author of the Cadence of Grace series and *This Quiet Sky*, has a deep passion for writing stories that shine light on God's grace and goodness. She lives in the mountains of Southern California with her husband and their three children, just a few minutes from a feed store where her husband grew up helping run his family's Christmas tree lot. You can find her at joannebischof.com. For more of Riley and Becca's story, watch for Joanne's novel *To Get to You*.

8

The Last Ember

by Linda Bonney Olin

Karen sighed as she stared at the line of customers waiting for her to ring up their last-minute Christmas purchases. They looked as fretful and exhausted as she felt.

"How are you today?" she droned.

"Very well, thank you. And you?" A note of genuine interest in the thin voice claimed Karen's attention. The tweed-coated, fuzzy-hatted lady at her register seemed to actually be waiting for an answer.

"I'm fine, thanks." Karen slid the woman's shopping basket down the counter. Clenching her jaw against the pain flaring in her shoulder, she lifted out a small wooden stable with painted figures of Mary, Joseph, the manger, and a few barn animals glued inside. It was heavier than it looked.

"Isn't it delightful?" The woman's smile stretched the wrinkles in her cheeks nearly to her red poinsettia earrings.

Karen rotated the nativity in her hands. "Mm … I don't see a price tag."

A gnarled finger pointed. "It was on the—" The woman's wrist bumped Karen's, and the stable crashed onto the counter, splintering the roof. A tiny block of colored wood bounced away.

Karen gasped. "I'm so sorry!"

"My fault entirely." The woman stepped back to scan the area around her feet. "But where did that little rascal roll to?"

The customer beside her, a man in his thirties with a tall, rugged build, touched her coat sleeve. "Let me look." He dropped to one knee and felt around the floor. Shoppers behind him let out a chorus of groans and rude comments. Several switched to a faster-moving line, clashing their loaded carts like bumper cars.

Karen shot a panicky look around the checkout area for Mr. Penwick. He'd already written her up for zoning out at her register after pain in her arm kept her awake two nights in a row. If he cut her hours as punishment for broken merchandise and brawling customers, she'd never dig out from under the debts Thomas had left behind.

"Hold on. … Got it!" The man jumped up, a grin deepening the laugh lines around his wide hazel eyes, and handed Karen the missing piece.

"Ah," the old lady said. "Baby Jesus came unglued."

Karen fought a nervous giggle. *He's not the only one.* "I'll get another set off the shelf."

More moans from the backed-up line.

"Oh, no, I'd rather mend this one. I'll cherish it all the more for its bumps and bruises."

Karen resisted a roll of her eyes. No one was likely to cherish *her* more for her scars.

The young man pointed. "And there's the price tag, stuck to the side of your shopping basket."

"Ha! Thank You, Lord!" The woman unclasped her purse.

Karen applied a steep discount to the damaged goods and gave the beaming woman her standard send-off. "Thank you. Have a nice evening."

"Thank *you*, my dear. Have a special Christmas Eve!" She leaned closer and pressed a business card into Karen's palm. "I'll be praying for you," she murmured. "And if you'd like to chat, you can call me." She took her bag and toddled off through the crowd.

"Wait for me, Gram!" The tall man hastily paid for his peanut brittle, wished Karen a blessed Christmas, and caught up with the old woman. He shouldered her bag, offered his arm, and held the door open for her. His tender smile lit a spark of joy in Karen's heart.

A twinge of regret stabbed her too. Her husband had treated her tenderly once. But Thomas had returned from two tours in Afghanistan a different man, volatile and abusive. She flexed her injured arm and winced.

"Hey, miss! We're waiting!"

Karen's rote "How are you today?" prompted an angry earful from that customer and the next. So it went, until the last shopper hurried away right at closing time.

Mr. Penwick intercepted Karen at the door with an envelope. A Christmas bonus, perhaps? She ripped it open. A layoff slip, effective immediately.

The spark of joy was all but extinguished.

Snow fell in sparse, dry flakes as Karen trudged up the steps of her run-down Victorian rental. The store didn't need as many cashiers now that the Christmas rush was over. She got that. But what was she supposed to live on? Fear tightened her throat. What would the creditors do when her payments stopped?

Inside, a pall of chilly air welcomed her home. The furnace must have run dry. Without money, she couldn't buy more fuel oil.

A lamp in the living room faintly illuminated the Christmas cards on the mantel. Karen crumpled the mocking holiday scenes and tossed them into the fireplace. She steepled the last few logs on top and ignited the pile. Pulling close the tatty afghan her mother had knit as a long-ago Christmas present, she slumped onto the couch to watch the flames dance.

Dancing flames were an illusion, of course. A lot of snap and crackle, a little light and warmth, and then nothing. Life was like that. So was love. Karen's once-shining hopes had burned down to their last embers. Soon they'd be as cold and dead as Thomas.

And so would she.

She'd visualized this moment, quite often lately. Tonight she would quit fantasizing and do it. She slid a backpack from behind the couch and drew out the contents, arranging the bottles in a neat line on the coffee table. Painkillers. Antidepressants. Sleeping pills. And a nice chardonnay to wash them all down. Thomas had put an end to his exhaustion, pain, and nightmares with a pharmaceutical cocktail. His recipe would be her escape too.

She uncorked the wine and raised a toast. "Rest in peace, Karen!"

She took a long gulp. As she set the bottle on the coffee table, she knocked over a small pill container. It skittered across the cracked wooden floor, reminding her of the baby Jesus figurine and the hazel-eyed man who'd rescued it. Karen would never have a second chance at happiness with a considerate man like that. She was damaged goods now, just like the broken stable.

She retrieved the container, swallowed the painkillers, and drank deeply. When she leaned forward to set the wine bottle back on the table, something in her jeans pocket jabbed her thigh. It was the corner of that tweedy little grandmother's business card. She pulled it out.

Frances Dean. Local address. Only a few streets away, in fact. A radiant cross shone in the background. Maybe she was like those Scripture-spouters who always pressed Karen to join their church while she rang up their purchases.

But Frances had offered prayers. And conversation. Karen thought she might enjoy that. But it was too late. Good church ladies would all be tucked into their beds at this hour, especially on Christmas Eve.

The embers in the fireplace turned to ash while handful after handful of pills sluiced down Karen's throat. She chugged the chardonnay, not caring that it dribbled on her shirt. After downing the last sleeping tablet, she shook each pill container. Nothing rattled inside. Lifting the wine bottle for a last drink didn't hurt her shoulder. The drugs were starting to do their job.

She fingered Frances Dean's card. Maybe the woman had an answering machine. Karen liked the idea of leaving a message for her to hear on Christmas morning. *Hello and good-bye. Thanks for not blaming me for the broken stable, even though I lost my job anyway.*

After wrapping herself in the afghan, Karen carried the telephone from the end table to the couch and dialed.

"Hello?"

No answering machine. "Oh. Umm … Mrs. Dean? This is Karen Taylor. From the store?"

"How lovely to hear from you, Karen." Warmth flooded the frail voice. "Please, call me Fran."

"Sorry to bother you so late."

"Oh, I often stay awake till the wee hours. I do my best praying at night."

"Me too. The awake part, I mean. Sometimes I pray too. But I'm not very good at it. I usually just ask God to fix me."

"That's a perfect prayer. Especially at Christmas. God sent His Son to fix this broken world and all the broken people in it. No matter who we are or what we've done."

"Yeah, about that. I'm sorry I broke your …" Her fuzzy brain groped for the word. "Your nava-tivity."

"Oh, my grandson repaired it with a spot of glue. It was you that concerned us, my dear. You looked so worn out."

"Oh, don't worry about me." Karen yawned, not even trying to hide it. The pills and alcohol were definitely taking effect. "I'll be fine. Very soon. I juss called to say Merry Christmas before I go. And to thank you for bein' so nice."

"Karen?" Fran's voice sharpened. "Where are you going, dear?"

"Juss … away."

"Are you at home now?"

"Uh-huh."

"Give me your address. I—I'd like to send you a Christmas gift."

"Too late."

"It's never too late for Christmas. Karen, what street do you live on?"

Karen wasn't sure whether she answered aloud or only in her mind. As if from far away, the telephone receiver thumped to the floor. Her limp body followed.

The impact jolted her awake. Her throat felt parched. She tried to reach for the wine bottle, but her arm wouldn't move. She wept at her powerlessness.

She heard pounding, and her name echoed in the distance. Why was an icy wind blowing through the house? Her body shook.

"Stay with me, Karen," a strong voice pleaded.

She struggled to focus on the lamp-lit hazel eyes staring into hers.

An ember of hope glowed.
It's never too late for Christmas.

Life Application

"Unless the Lord had given me help, I would soon have dwelt in the silence of death" (Psalm 94:17). When Karen's emotional, physical, and financial devastation led her to attempt suicide, the Lord's help came in the form of two kind strangers who reached out in prayer and in person. Their selflessness in action reflects that of Jesus, who left the comforts of His heavenly home and came into our broken world to save us.

Helping a hurting individual sometimes means entering an unfamiliar, distressing world. Are we willing to leave behind our own comforts and concerns and say, "I'll go! Send me" (see Isaiah 6:8)?

About the Author

Linda Bonney Olin writes hymns, drama scripts, poems, devotions—whatever the Holy Spirit assigns. Her books include *Songs for the Lord* and *Transformed: 5 Resurrection Dramas*. Linda and Bill, her husband of forty-plus years, live on their farm in upstate New York. Visit her Faith Songs website, LindaBonneyOlin.com.

9

Sculpting a Perfect Gift

by Mary Kay Moody

Liz fussed and fumed as she shuffled across the snow-covered driveway of Haven's Home, trying to keep up with her hyperactive five-year-old and the three boisterous teenagers who'd dropped their bags on the steps and started pitching snowballs at each other. They'd better not toss any her way. With her arms piled high, that would be the last straw. Skit props and refreshments would tumble, and she would turn around and go home, despite her sister's plans for their children to yet again put on the Christmas show they'd been performing for Haven residents for the past six years.

Six years. Hard to believe her mother had begun disappearing into a fog so long ago, yet her shell kept going. Liz and her siblings had tried everything to keep Mother in her own home. When that failed, they attempted to draw her out of the haze by telling stories along with photo albums, suggesting activities to keep her mind sharp, taking her for visits with friends, engaging in her favorite games, sports, and music. Occasionally she seemed coherent, though less often recently.

Now the siblings arranged the Christmas holidays so that at least one of them visited her each day. Liz huffed. Yesterday was her day. Today she was *supposed* to be cooking and preparing her house for the Christmas party. Yet here she was again, this time dragging bags of junk to help her nieces and nephew put on their goofy holiday skits.

Lord, I feel like Martha preparing her meal for Jesus. Couldn't You send someone to help me?

"Aunt Liz, let me carry that big bag." Jay wrinkled his nose. "Sorry I didn't offer before."

She let the weight fall off her arm onto his.

Davey bounded up the steps.

"Wipe your feet, Son," Liz hollered. This was going to be a long afternoon.

Inside, she got Davey settled at a corner table by himself. She covered it with a plastic tablecloth, gave him his box of modeling clay, and tousled his blond head. "Will you be okay here while I help your cousins?"

"Sure, Mom," he said, grabbing a bright red block.

"Please don't leave this spot."

"I won't." He rolled the clay into a log.

Liz helped the teens drape a sheet between two lamps to make a curtain, then sorted hats, a blow-up snowman, a cardboard fireplace, huge lawn candy canes, and other props, placing them in order on a table.

She stretched her back and peeked around. The room was

filling with residents—some wheeled in, others with walkers straggling toward empty chairs. So many faces were blank; only a few appeared excited. Liz wondered if the canned Christmas music playing over the intercom had faded into background noise for most of these folks.

She waved as Mother was escorted to a seat. Not a spark of recognition.

Seeing her once-vibrant mother like this became harder every time. Perhaps she'd cut her visits back, freeing up a couple of hours each week. They did no good anyway.

Jay, wearing an elf hat, stepped in front of the curtain and banged two pot lids together like cymbals. "Hear ye, hear ye! Our carolers wish you a Merry Christmas!"

On cue, Sophie and Emma joined him and the show was on. Megan had been right. Her kids *could* pull off this show without assistance. Liz leaned against the wall and scanned the sea of faces. More displayed smiles and lively eyes now, though only three sang along. Mother resembled a wax statue—unmoving, unseeing.

Is that even living?

Across the room, Davey walked toward the audience, dipping and swirling his red clay plane in the air. Liz waved for him to go back, but he kept walking, engrossed in his toy, finally stopping at Mother's side. Leaning close, he spoke to her and held out his airplane.

Poor kid. He's picked the wrong person to get some praise from.

Mother appeared to study the object, then took it from his

hand. *Oh, no!* For all Liz knew, the woman might eat it. She bolted, but had only gone two steps when Sophie tugged on her arm.

"Aunt Liz, I need help," she whispered. "I have to change costumes and my zipper's stuck."

Liz glanced at her mother, who was staring at the airplane in her hand, then turned to her niece and worked the zipper free.

"Thanks." Sophie ripped off her ski jacket and strode to the prop table.

Liz glanced back at Mother—she was mashing Davey's plane. Liz dashed along the wall and across the back of the room. She couldn't move fast enough. Within seconds Davey would start shrieking and disrupt the entertainment. When chaos broke out, distracting the residents' attention, she would never hear the end of Megan's lament about how Liz had ruined the Christmas show for the Haven residents.

Davey walked back to his table, picked up another hunk of clay, and returned to his grandmother. He stood quietly at her side and watched as she squeezed clay through her fingers. A scrap fell to the floor. He picked it up, then clasped Mother's hand and tugged her up. Slowly she rose and followed him to the table, then sat in his chair.

He nudged more clay fragments toward her and talked softly as he rolled a scrap of yellow clay between his palms.

Mother reached for a brown piece and began working it.

"Your fingers are strong, Grandma."

Tears clouded Liz's vision. At the sight of the long,

once-straight fingers shaping and smoothing clay, memories rose up and crashed over her like a tidal wave. Memories of her mother, young and lively, standing at her art table, sculpting statues of Liz and Megan. While they modeled their own crude figures, she peppered them with praise for their patience, their beauty, their kindness to each other. Mother never ran out of compliments and encouraging observations.

As Jay and Emma sang "O Tannenbaum," Liz glanced their way. Sophie pirouetted across the stage, draped in a full-length dark-green skirt and billowy green poncho, festooned with garland and bejeweled ornaments—no doubt her attempt to look like a *tannenbaum*. The gold umbrella hat atop her head was apparently supposed to look like a tree-topper star.

"Here, Grandma." Davey passed Mother some green clay and kept up a soft-spoken narrative as she massaged the green blob.

While staff members dressed as elves passed out homemade cookies, Liz watched Mother's fingers work the clay, softening and molding, then accepting another color from Davey.

"Boy, Grandma, you're fast. I can't make faces as good as you. Would you teach me?"

Liz held her breath, wondering which of these two people she loved would be pushed beyond the breaking point first.

"Most people think heads are round, David, but they're not. See?" She formed an oval. "Then you pinch the jaw in a bit. Scoop tiny indents for the eyes, and add a lump on each cheek, then smooth it forward like this." Voilà, a nose appeared.

"Wow," he breathed.

"You want to try?"

"I'll watch you a few more times."

Mother laughed. The sound that used to lilt was now a bit raspy. But a laugh! Liz hadn't heard that joyful noise in over a year.

Davey passed Mother his orb of yellow. "Make a star, Grandma."

Mother fashioned a star, then pinched it atop the clay evergreen tree standing at the head of the crèche she'd just sculpted. Meanwhile, the teenagers sang and distributed cookies, unaware that in a corner of the room a miracle was taking place.

Davey grinned up at Liz as she approached the twosome and rested a hand on each one's shoulder. "Mother," she said, her voice cracking, "that's lovely."

A warm, gnarled hand patted hers. "Thank you, Liz. And Merry Christmas."

Life Application

Scripture says that when the Messiah was born "they shall call his name Emmanuel, which being interpreted is, God with us" (Matthew 1:23 KJV). God's presence with us is an astonishing gift. He can meet whatever need we have. In ways beyond any we can imagine, God uses everything, no matter how tattered or stressed, to weave our life tapestry and bless us in unexpected ways.

God has also given us the gift of choice. Along the path of our days, we're blessed with myriad opportunities to make decisions. God exercised His choice by allowing the Messiah to pay for our sins so we don't have to. We have the freedom to either accept or reject His Son—an incomparable gift.

How often do we choose our own priorities and miss some unique blessings God has put on a path we refuse to walk? As we travel through our lives, I pray we will all have the willingness to choose God's path, eyes to observe the blessings He rains down, and childlike hearts to dive into them.

About the Author

Mary Kay Moody is a freelance writer with a passion for exploring life at the startling intersection of our plans and God's purposes. Visit her website, marykaymoody.com, or connect with her on Facebook.

10

The Box

by Jan Cline

Christine cupped her hand against the icy storefront window. She pressed her forehead on the cold glass, her breath making a circle of steam that melted the frost. She scanned the entire display. The spot where the box had been the day before was now empty. She held her breath, examining the shelves beyond, but the box wasn't there. Perhaps it had been moved to another place in the sundry shop.

Oh Lord, please don't let it be gone. She pulled away from the glass and watched it frost over again.

Christine pushed open the heavy glass-paned door and stepped into the store. She breathed in the sweet, musty smells of old books and fabric bolts. Her eyes were drawn to the massive shelves that reached to the ceiling, stuffed with box upon box of merchandise. To her right, a long display cabinet glistened with trinkets and fine jewelry, sparkling like stars.

Several customers rifled through piles of woolen hats and mittens in a bin beneath a sign that read "Christmas Sale."

The white-haired shopkeeper stared down at her from behind the case. "Can I help you find something?" Bushy black brows crowned his dark eyes. His crisp green apron and a bright red bow tie reminded her of Santa Claus.

She crept toward him with shaking knees. "Yes, sir."

He leaned in. "Well, speak up, child. What do you need? Are you here to pick up something for your mother?"

In a way it was true, but she didn't have time to explain. "No, sir. I was wondering what happened to the silver jewelry box that was in your window. The one with a red gem on the top." She held her breath.

"Oh, yes. I know the one you mean. I sold it just this morning."

Christine fought back stinging tears. Why didn't she visit the shop yesterday instead of waiting till Christmas Eve? Now she'd lost her chance.

"I have lots of other nice things. Look at the wooden toys over there on the shelf and see if you find something you like." A smile softened his expression, but the ache in her heart only intensified.

"No, thank you." Christine shuffled out the door, letting the tears fall.

The cold wind stung her face before she could pull her scarf up.

"Oh, Mama, I wanted so much to buy you that box." After watching her mother admire it in the window weeks ago, she planned to give it to her for Christmas. Devising her presentation had dominated her thoughts and daydreams as the holiday drew closer.

After sweeping Mrs. Miller's porch that morning, she had rushed to the shop with cash in hand. But it was too late. All the pennies she had saved for weeks working odd jobs after school still jingled in her pocket.

She stepped into the candy shop next door and bought a box of dark chocolates. "Will you please tie it with a pretty red bow?" The woman behind the counter winked when she handed her the little box, dressed up with curly ribbon.

Christine drifted home, crying the tears she didn't want her mother to see. She looked to the night sky. "Lord, Mama deserves better than a box of candy. It's been so dark in our house since Papa died." The sting of grief and poverty made the whole world seem bleak and unfair.

Large snowflakes fell like feathers as she made her way up the stoop to the flat. A soft glow filtered through the frosted window. Mama must be home from work early.

"Psst. Christine." Mrs. MacGregor leaned out the second-story window, pulling her sweater tight under her chin.

"Merry Christmas, Mrs. MacGregor."

"Come up here," the old woman called to her. "I have something for you."

Christine went inside and hung her snow-covered cloak on a brass hook in the hall. She took the steps two by two. Her mouth watered as she thought about Mrs. MacGregor's moist fruitcake, which she'd given to Papa every year. He hated fruitcake, but he always thanked her and brought it home to Christine and Mama, who savored it for days.

Mrs. MacGregor stood in the hall by her door, holding out her offering.

"Thank you, ma'am." Christine took the package. It was much too small to be fruitcake.

"Your father gave this to me for safekeeping months ago. It's a gift for your mother."

A gift from Papa to Mama? What could it be? Tears stung her eyes.

Mrs. MacGregor gave her a hug. "Don't let your mother see you cry. Your father would want you to enjoy your Christmas."

Christine dreaded each step down the stairs. Surely Papa's gift would make Mama cry too.

When Christine stepped into the parlor, she saw her mother standing by the window, a mischievous sparkle in her eyes. A small, spindly tree sat atop the table beside her. Twinkling candles dripped wax on branches adorned with strings of cranberries and paper angels. Where had that tree come from?

Christine moved closer, clutching the meager box of chocolates and Papa's package. As she neared her mother, something under the tree reflected the candlelight, catching her eye. Christine moved closer to it. A little silver jewelry box with a shiny red gem on the top lay nestled under the tree.

"Mama, what's this?"

"It's for you." She reached for the box. "I saw you admiring it in the shop window."

A stream of tears fell. "And these are for you." Christine held out both gifts. "One is from me, the other is from … Papa."

Mama opened Papa's gift first. A shiny silver medallion dangled from a delicate chain. She held it in the air and let it spin in the candlelight. "It's just like your father to do this." She opened the jewelry box. "Will you keep it for me in here?"

"It's the perfect place." She dropped the necklace inside. "You'll always know where it is whenever you need it."

Arm in arm, they stood admiring the tree. Papa was there after all.

"We'll be fine, won't we, Mama?"

"Yes. Except for one thing."

Christine frowned. "What?"

Mama smirked. "No fruitcake this year."

They both laughed. "Maybe she sent it up to Papa in heaven," Christine said.

She placed the jewelry box on her dresser between Papa's picture and her Sunday school Bible. The quilts piled high on her bed felt especially warm that night. She closed her eyes, envisioning her father in heaven.

"Good night, Papa. I hope you enjoy the fruitcake."

She giggled before sleep closed her eyes.

Life Application

We all treasure the giving of presents at Christmas. It warms our hearts to see the joy in people's eyes when we hand them even a small token. The experience is like that of the Father's when He bestows gifts of love, peace, and unimaginable grace—though on a grander scale.

God knows who should get what gifts. He carefully designs and fashions everything He gives, with our welfare in mind. If we look closely, we may discover a special surprise waiting for us under the tree this year.

About the Author

Jan Cline has written numerous articles, short stories, and devotionals. She is the founder and director of the Inland NW Christian Writers Conference and speaks to women's groups and writers' groups.

11

Star Light, Star Bright

by Kathy Ide

Joseph sat on a pile of hay, gazing at the sphere of light that illuminated the night sky. It shone so brightly, he could make out every piece of straw outside the cave entrance, every hair on the mane of the donkey Mary had been riding when she went into labor.

"Mary, you've got to see this." He rushed back into the dark shelter, but stopped when he saw her asleep on the makeshift bed he'd hastily assembled after the innkeeper led them here last night.

And why shouldn't she sleep, after what she'd been through? He sat on the ground beside his beloved, aching to share the thoughts that had been tumbling around in his mind ever since … well, ever since that angel appeared to him in a dream. "It's been an incredible night, hasn't it?" he whispered.

She didn't stir. Didn't move at all, other than the gentle rise and fall of her chest.

"Mary." Her name felt soft on his lips. "Now that it's all over, I have a confession to make. I'm … I'm scared." Watching her give birth had been the most frightening thing he'd ever experienced. No wonder men were not traditionally allowed to watch the natural but gruesome ordeal of a woman in travail.

But what he felt now was a completely different kind of fear.

He crossed to the feeding trough, which he'd spent hours cleaning and recleaning, packing and repacking with the freshest hay he could find—the only thing he'd been able to think of to do to keep sane during Mary's labor. There, wrapped tight in swaddling cloths, lay the child that she had delivered into his arms.

But Joseph was not the boy's father.

He averted his eyes from the newborn. After all, no one could look on the face of God and live.

He turned instead toward Mary. "Adonai, I understand why You chose her—out of all the women who have ever lived—to be the mother of Your only child. She's so good and kind and godly. She loves You more than anyone I've ever known. That's why *I* love her."

A thought entered his mind in a split moment of time—as gentle as a sigh yet as powerful as a storm.

I chose you, too, Joseph.

He gasped at the thought. Why would the Lord Shaddai choose him, a lowly carpenter, to raise His only Son? To be the earthly father of the long-awaited Messiah?

"I have nothing to offer. My biggest goal in life was to teach my child the business my father taught me. What does the Son of God need with a mundane skill like that?"

Joseph's gaze returned to the feeding trough. Unable to resist the pull, he dared risk a peek at the newborn's face. Once his eyes landed on the wrinkly red cheeks and sparse brown hair, he could not turn away. The baby looked so … ordinary.

Could this child truly be what the angel had told Joseph and Mary He would be?

It wasn't that Joseph doubted the divine dream. It was far too incredible and vivid to have been merely his imagination. But this was all wrong. His whole life the rabbis—and his own father—had taught him the Messiah would be a mighty warrior king who would free His people from their oppressors.

Throughout Mary's pregnancy, Joseph had tried to envision what the Son of God would look like when He was born. Surely He would be unique right from birth. He'd be able to walk and talk straight from the womb. All right, that was a bit of a stretch. But shouldn't He at least have a heavenly glow about Him? A radiance that beamed from His holy face, like Moses when he came down from Mount Sinai? *Something* that set Him apart, leaving no question in anyone's mind about who and what this child really was.

And yet … the sleeping child before him looked just like any other newborn. The only thing different about this birth was that extra-bright star that appeared above this cave moments after Mary's delivery.

Joseph's heart sank. When he and Mary returned home

with a normal-looking baby, everyone would discount the stories of their angelic visitations. All the vicious rumors would be confirmed.

He stared at the infant, longing to draw near, to pick him up, to hold him. Yet he hesitated. Could anyone really cradle God in his arms? Especially someone as unworthy as he?

Unable to fathom the enormity of this bizarre situation, Joseph fled the cave and paced outside it.

He stared again at the brilliant star above him. Such an unusual light. People for miles around must be able to see it. What did those who studied astrological formations think of it?

A rustling in the dry brush startled him. The innkeeper had moved his domestic animals to a pen. So it wasn't a cow or donkey or sheep that had made the noise. A wild animal, perhaps?

With all the people crowded into this little town, bandits were no doubt roaming the outskirts, eager to take advantage of anyone who let his guard down.

Then another thought chilled him to the depths of his soul. Perhaps the danger came not from man but from spiritual forces of evil and darkness. Surely they would try to strike at the Son of God while He was a vulnerable infant. How on earth could Joseph even begin to protect Jesus from that?

The sound grew louder. Footsteps. Human footsteps. Dozens of them.

Joseph looked around for anything he might use as a defensive weapon. A rock. A staff. A thick tree limb. But found nothing. *What do I do? God, help us!* Surely He would protect

His child. But did that banner of protection cover him and Mary as well? Or were their parts of the miraculous story over?

A reeking stench of manure filled Joseph's nose as men dressed in crudely made woolen garments moved into the open.

Shepherds.

Joseph fought an instinctive reaction of judgment and condemnation. With a few exceptions—tax collecting and prostitution came to mind—shepherding was the lowest profession an Israelite could choose. Why would anyone spend months at a time wandering the hillsides herding stubborn animals that didn't have the common sense to find their own grass or stay out of brambles or keep from tumbling into pits? And shepherds rarely had time to attend synagogue … which was just as well since they'd find little acceptance there.

"Please excuse the interruption," said the first man in the group, his weather-worn face covered in wrinkles and scars. "But … angels told us to come here."

Joseph swallowed hard. The Lord had chosen two average people to be the parents of His holy Son. Apparently He had deigned to deliver the news of that child's birth not to kings and nobles, or religious leaders who had studied the messianic prophecies so diligently for so long, but to the lowliest of the low. And Joseph was no better than these shepherds—how dare he judge them when God had so blessed them?

"Welcome, gentlemen. You've come to the right place. Wait here a moment, please." He ducked into the cave, eager to share the amazing miracle with the people God had personally invited to see it.

He knelt beside his betrothed and gently tugged on the rough blanket that covered her. Her eyes fluttered open. “Mary, my love, we have our first visitors. I’ll go out and talk with them while you get yourself and the baby ready.”

Mary had managed to stay awake for their first guests, and of course she’d been kind and gracious to them. But the effort had taken its toll, and she fell asleep soon after their departure.

When the child cried—and stank—Joseph forced himself to overcome a lifetime of strict instruction not to touch anything deemed holy and changed the Son of God’s soiled swaddling cloths. His mind still reeled.

As he held the tiny, helpless baby in his arms, a rush of emotion engulfed him. As much as he loved Mary, this feeling ran even deeper and stronger. He couldn’t take his eyes off the precious bundle in his arms. Nor could he stop his forefinger from gently stroking the soft skin of those pudgy little cheeks.

“Jesus, fathers are supposed to teach their children everything they need to know. But what can I teach You? You’ve already shown me more than I’ll ever be able to show You. You’ve taught me about … miracles. God’s infinite power. His overwhelming love for mankind. What can I offer You in return? Nothing!”

Nothing but love.

Joseph sucked in a quick breath, the realization hitting him like a plank over the head. “Oh, Jesus, if that is what You need from me—love—I can give You that in abundance!”

Perhaps God had made the right choice after all.

He held the babe tighter to his chest. "Sweet little Jesus. I can hold You when You cry. I can provide food and shelter." Joseph chuckled. "Mary and I don't live like King Herod, mind you. But our home is a far cry better than this stable!"

He grinned at the infant in his arms. "Wait till you see our place, Jesus. My father and I built the house, and Mary's done a wonderful job of making it feel like home."

His exhausted bride stirred, and Joseph took the child outside. "Jesus, I don't know what kind of father I'll be. But I promise You … and all the angels watching us right now … that with the help of our heavenly Father, I will love You and Your mother with all my heart, all my strength, and all my soul, every day of my life."

He looked up into the brilliantly lit night sky. "Thank You, Lord, for the awesome privilege and responsibility You've bestowed on me. And thank You for placing a special star in the heavens to unmistakably guide all who see it to Your strange but amazing plan to save the world."

Life Application

God provided the way to reconcile sinful man with His holy presence: by becoming a human being Himself. Like the star that accompanied that auspicious occasion, Jesus spent thirty-three years lighting the way, telling us—and showing us—what God is like and how much He loves us. Then He died on the cross and rose again, to become the bridge we need to enter into the Father's presence and have Him see us as just as holy and righteous as His own Son.

And yet … often we view God as being too big, too holy, too powerful for us to even consider approaching Him. We feel too small, too sinful, too unimportant for God to be interested in the insignificant details of our fleeting lives.

Other times, if we're honest, we may view ourselves as being perfectly capable of handling our own lives without any divine help—or interference.

I'm sure Joseph didn't feel worthy of being the earthly father to God's only begotten Son. But I'm equally certain that he and Mary loved Jesus with all their hearts. And that's really all that God the Father wanted them to do.

That's also what He wants us to do. Simply love Him.

About the Author

Kathy Ide, author of *Proofreading Secrets of Best-Selling Authors*, is a freelance editor/mentor for new writers, established authors, and book publishers. She speaks at writers' conferences across the country. She is the founder and director of The Christian PEN and the Christian Editor Connection. For more, visit KathyIde.com.

12

A Present Hope

by Lynn Kinnaman

Tina hated parallel parking. Finding an empty place on the narrow streets added to her list of irritations in an already annoying day. To say she wasn't in the mood for the annual office party would be an understatement. She wasn't in the mood for Christmas.

Every year it started earlier. The Santas. The sales. The controversy over saying "Happy Holidays" or "Merry Christmas." The unrelenting push to buy, buy, buy. Advertisers even urged people to get things for themselves. One for you, two for me. It had become a feeding frenzy.

Tina had fallen for the relentless pitch and bought something for herself this year. The winter coat she'd had her eye on for months had been slashed to half price, and she'd snapped it up.

Well, at least this party had finally given her the opportunity to wear it.

The get-together was in a high-demand area within walking distance of the university. Parking as well as property was at a premium here, so she felt lucky when she found a spot close by, even if it took her three tries to get wedged in place.

She grabbed her $10-and-under gift and got out of the car, careful to avoid the patches of ice on her way to the house. She heard Christmas music playing inside as she rang the bell.

Darcy opened the door. “Tina! Come in!”

She entered, stuffing her gloves into her pockets.

“Here, I’ll take your coat.”

She slipped it off.

“It’s beautiful.”

“Thanks.” Since the divorce, Tina didn’t have much in the way of special treats in her life. Her days were made up of earning a living, paying the bills, and trying to eat right and exercise. The last two were a joke, but remained on her to-do list in the hopes that their sheer presence would work miracles.

So far that plan had been a bust.

The new coat helped offset her depression.

“Your house is lovely.”

The place screamed Christmas. But it was easy to surround yourself with holiday cheer when your husband made good money and you had nothing better to do all day than put up decorations.

The next three hours passed pleasantly, and the day’s frustrations faded in the upbeat company.

When she rose to leave, the chorus of protestations was

gratifying but meaningless. Tina had been on the other side. She knew the remaining guests would resume without a pause.

Tina located the guest room, where coats were piled on the bed. After finding hers, she escaped into the night and returned to her car.

Falling snow interfered with visibility. Smart people were home by now, not out on the dark streets. She turned on the wipers, but they smeared instead of swept the snowflakes away.

When she saw a figure dart across the road, her foot smashed the brake pedal. She got out and saw someone on the ground. She ran to the prostrate young woman. "Are you okay?"

"I'm fine."

"I didn't hit you, did I?" She hadn't felt an impact.

"No. I slipped on the ice." She tried to get up. "Ow."

Tina helped the woman stand. "Do you think you broke something?"

"I hope not. But it does hurt."

"Do you need to go to the hospital?"

"No. I'll be fine."

"Can I take you somewhere else then?"

"I was on my way to the grocery store. Would you mind—"

"Not at all." As Tina helped her to the car, she noticed how cold and wet the hoodie was that the girl wore over her jeans. "I'm Tina."

"Reese."

As they drove the couple of blocks to the market, Tina learned that Reese was a first-year college student and lived in the dorms down the street.

When they pulled up in front of the grocery store, Reese thanked her. Tina noticed her favoring her right ankle as she made her way to the door.

She lowered the window and leaned out. "Go inside and wait for me. I'll come in as soon as I park." Before Reese could respond, Tina pulled into a parking spot. When she got into the store, the girl was holding a small basket.

"I appreciate your concern, but I don't really need your help."

"If you walk much on that ankle, you could make it worse." Tina took the basket and exchanged it for a shopping cart. "Get whatever you need, then I'll give you a ride to your dorm."

She flashed a grateful smile. "Thanks."

They went down the aisles together. Reese checked the price on every item, choosing only what was on sale or discounted.

"Do you have family nearby?" Tina asked, trying to sound casual.

"My parents live in Montana. My sister's in New York."

"Are you going home for Christmas?"

"Not this year. I work part time to pay for books and groceries. But I can't afford a plane ticket."

"Is your family coming here then?"

Reese evaluated the selection of granola bars, taking two boxes after careful consideration. "My mom is sick and my dad has to take care of her."

Tina didn't know what to say.

"I'm sorry. I don't usually tell strangers my life story."

"It's okay. I just wish I could help."

Dimples popped out on Reese's cheeks. "You are helping."

At the dorm, Tina followed Reese, carrying the two bags. Her room was on the third floor. It was a long, slow climb. The girl shivered with every step.

Halfway down the hall, Reese opened a door and took the bags. "Thank you so much for your kindness."

"Why don't you let me put those things away while you take a warm shower."

"I'd appreciate that."

"And don't hurry to finish. I can let myself out."

After putting Reese's purchases into the cupboards, Tiny knew she should leave. But she wanted to do more. She had some cash in her purse, but it was in the car. Besides, cash seemed impersonal. Even offensive.

She took off her coat. The one indulgence she'd purchased for herself this Christmas. She laid it on the couch. Finding a piece of scratch paper and a pen, she wrote:

Reese,

I want you to have this.

Best of luck with your studies. I know you'll make your parents proud.

I'd love to have you join me for Christmas dinner. Here's my phone number.

Tina

"Merry Christmas, Reese," she whispered as she pulled the door closed.

Life Application

We enjoy giving gifts to those we love. The more we love them, the harder we try to find something that will convey our love.

John 3:16–17 says, "For God so loved the world that he gave his one and only Son, that whoever believes in him shall not perish but have eternal life. For God did not send his Son into the world to condemn the world, but to save the world through him."

What better gift could we ever receive?

By celebrating the birth of the baby Jesus, we are acknowledging the priceless gift God gave to us. No matter who we are, what we've done, or where we've been, our generous God has given us the hope of eternal life. And with that hope, our lives overflow with opportunities to help others.

About the Author

Lynn Kinnaman has been publishing fiction and nonfiction for more than thirty years. She's the author of the Comfort Verses devotional series, the RV Travel Mysteries series, and other fiction, travel, and informational books. She is also the editor of *SW Montana Magazine* and organizer for the annual Get Published Conference for Writers. She lives in Montana near her daughters and their families. Find out more at LynnKinnaman.com.

13

A Violet Christmas

by Summer Robidoux

Violet's blue eyes twinkled like the red and green lights on the Christmas tree, a huge smile covering her tiny face. Anne couldn't help but grin at her daughter's enthusiasm.

This day had started as a typical December Monday in Colorado: sunshine in the morning and a blizzard by noon. Anne barely got Violet off to school on time. On the last week before Christmas break, like the other twenty-four eager second graders in her class, Violet could barely contain her excitement. Anne felt sorry for their poor teacher.

She waved good-bye as her daughter danced off to her classroom. Anne eased her way out of the school parking lot and headed to work, driving carefully through the snowy streets as she switched from mother mode into professional mode.

At work, the lot was already full, so Anne had to settle for a spot in the far row. She was breathless after the long trek to the Skyway headquarters building, where she meticulously balanced their books. It was quarter-end and year-end, so this week was unbelievably busy. As usual, Anne felt overwhelmed.

She'd heard Christmas songs in the background for the last month, but the music was an afterthought. Her tree was up only because of Violet's nagging and because Anne felt it was her motherly duty. After all, she had more important things to worry about.

After walking through the marble-floored lobby, Anne entered the elevator and pushed the button for the ninth floor. Soon she was tossing her coat aside and warming up her computer. The hours flew by but Anne hardly noticed.

Until her office door flew open and her assistant rushed in.

"Oh, my gosh! I'm glad you're here. The school just called." The look of alarm on Margo's face made Anne's stomach drop. "They've taken Violet to the hospital."

"Why?"

Margo pressed her lips into a thin line and shrugged.

Anne lunged for her coat and ran out the door.

The twenty-minute drive to the hospital felt like hours. Anne wanted to scream with frustration at every red light. She finally made it to the emergency room.

"My daughter," she blurted as she flew through the door. "She was brought in today. I need to find her!"

The lady behind the admission desk had salted hair and a friendly demeanor. "What is her name?"

"Violet McMurry."

"Let me see." She typed on the keyboard. "She's in pre-op."

"Pre-op?"

"Please take a seat in the waiting room and fill out these permission forms. I'll let the doctor know you're here. Someone will be right out to speak with you."

Anne nodded numbly and shuffled her way to a chair. The words on the paperwork blurred and her hand trembled so much she could barely write.

"Ms. McMurry?"

Anne bolted out of her seat and met a woman in blue scrubs. Her face was highlighted by hints of laugh lines and rosy cheeks.

"I'm Anne McMurry."

"Hi. I'm Tara, Violet's nurse."

"What's going on? Is she okay?"

Tara nodded. "Her class was drinking hot cocoa and eating popcorn while watching a movie. Violet somehow inhaled a popcorn kernel. The school said she exhibited some choking signs and has been coughing regularly. We took an X-ray and found the kernel lying where the windpipe branches off to go into either lung."

Whoever heard of popcorn threatening a child's life?

"The kernel needs to be removed before it moves deeper into her lungs. Once you've signed those forms, we're going to place Violet under anesthesia and perform a relatively quick and simple procedure. We're not expecting any complications. I'll let you know as soon as it's over."

Anne nodded. "Thank you."

Tara took the clipboard, flashed her a reassuring smile, and left.

Anne dropped back into her chair with a thud. She stared blankly at the dingy white wall in front of her, feeling numb and disoriented. Could this be real? What if something happened to Violet? Medical complications occurred every day. An uncontrollable terror caught Anne's breath short.

This was not the way things were supposed to be. Violet was to grow up, become a doctor or lawyer, get married, have children, and live happily ever after. No parent should have to lose a child.

Anne's eyes clouded with tears. *Please, God! Keep my baby safe.*

A bright light caught Anne's attention. She shielded her eyes with her hand. Sunshine pouring through the window reflected off a large metallic crucifix hanging on the adjacent wall. As Anne studied the sculpture of Jesus hanging on the cross, His expression solemn, with blood trickling down His face, her fear dissipated.

Losing a child was certainly not the natural cycle of life. Yet God had known that He was going to lose His child, Jesus. He was actually the one who sacrificed Him. Why would He do such a thing?

As Anne thought about how Violet's eyes lit up whenever she spoke of Santa, gifts, and the magic of Christmas, the answer came to her. Jesus brought hope to the world … even where none could be found.

Over the next half hour, Anne reprioritized her life. God,

family, friends, and then work. She vowed to take back her Christmas joy by dumping the excess that had robbed her of peace and clarity. She would relish the little moments she so often overlooked and learn from Violet's childlike wonder. Most important, she was going to appreciate and spread the gift of hope God had given her.

"Ms. McMurry?"

Anne looked up and saw Tara standing in front of her with a large smile. "Violet did great. We removed the kernel, and she's in recovery now. We want to observe her for a few hours. Once she's cleared, you can take her home. You'll need to keep her calm tonight."

Anne stood, blew out a nervous breath, and wiped away a tear of joy. "Can I see her?"

Tara led Anne toward the recovery rooms. "Are you all ready for Christmas?" she asked lightheartedly.

Anne shook her head. "No, not yet."

"What do you have left to do?"

"Just about everything." Anne paused. "But nothing of real importance. Thanks to God, the hard part has already been done for me. The rest is just details."

"Here we are." Tara pulled back the curtain leading into the room.

Anne's precious angel lay in a bed that seemed huge for her little frame. Violet's eyes met hers and she smiled. "Hi, Mommy!" She sounded hoarse, her throat still rough from the procedure.

"Hi, baby. How are you feeling?"

"Good."

"You gave me quite a scare."

"Sorry, Mommy."

Anne beamed at her daughter. "The important thing is you're okay." She gave Violet a hug, trying to avoid all the medical equipment. "We're going to hang out here for a little while, and then we'll go home."

Violet's brows pulled up. "I don't have to go back to school?"

Anne chuckled. "Not today. I think we'll change into our pj's, turn on the fireplace, and cuddle in front of the Christmas tree."

"What about your job?"

Anne sat on the side of the bed. "Some things are going to change … starting with my schedule. I'm going to work at the office during your school hours and at home after your bedtime. I have more important things to do."

"Like me?"

"Exactly!"

Violet gave her a smile so large it made Anne snicker. She could almost feel God's light reflecting off her. She pulled her daughter close and prayed a silent prayer. *Thank You, Jesus, for showing me what Christmas is all about!*

Life Application

Our everyday lives can easily become consumed by tasks, and we can lose sight of what is really important. Between our children's activities, our social and work lives, and our need to do what is expected, our internal to-do lists can take over our lives. Our true priorities should be a pleasure, not a chore that receives nothing more than a mental checkmark.

At the beginning of each day, take a minute and write a list of things that need to be accomplished. What does it say about your priorities? Have you made time for what is really important? Do you have God time? How about family time? If you can answer yes to these questions, then you are truly glorifying God.

About the Author

Summer Robidoux graduated from Northwest Missouri State University with a BS in psychology/biology and received her DC from Cleveland Chiropractic College. She lives in northern Colorado with her husband and three young daughters. She likes to hike, play volleyball, and write. Her novels include *The Pull* and *Finding Love between the Lines*.

14

A Decree Went Out

by Barbara Curtis

Logan Mitchell had found the perfect gift. Or at least one big enough to salve his conscience.

He hefted the wood-and-leather ottoman onto the counter. "Could you wrap it?" he asked the salesgirl.

"I don't know if we have a box that big. Even if we do, all we have is plain brown paper. If you want Christmas paper, the Scouts have gift-wrapping stations at the department stores."

"Brown's fine. I'm in a hurry."

The girl chuckled. "Isn't everyone this time of year?"

Logan checked his watch. At this rate he'd have just enough time to drop the footstool off at the nursing home and spend maybe an hour catching up on his grandfather's past three years there. Then Logan would hightail it out of Dodge before his sister and her crew showed up at Granddad's old folks' home for their Christmas party.

The clerk studied the stool. "It might take a while to find a box to fit that."

"That's fine." It wasn't, but what choice did he have?

As she walked off, a Christmas carol drifted in from the mall hallway. "We three kings of Orient are, bearing gifts we traverse afar …"

Logan could relate. He'd driven more than six hours to get this gift rather than sending a check to his sister and telling her to pick out whatever, like he usually did. He wasn't a Scrooge. Not really. Investment brokering just kept him busy. Very busy. Yet he'd found time to pick out gifts for Caleb and Haley. Not that they'd remember him. The last time he saw his niece and nephew, they were maybe four and six.

Logan reached into his pants pocket to extract his wallet. As he opened it, he saw the note, written in pencil, that he'd hastily stuffed in there.

Will you be here this year? Please come if you can. I miss you. I love you. Granddad.

Logan swallowed hard. It might actually be fun seeing Caleb open his hundred-dollar Lego set and Haley unwrap her life-size doll. Maybe this year he'd stay for Granddad's party after all. Just for a few minutes.

What was he thinking? He didn't have time for Christmas cheer.

On the fourth stanza of the carol, the clerk showed up with a box. She set it and the footstool on the floor. "After I take care of these other customers, I'll wrap it for you."

Didn't she understand his urgency? Logan eyed the elderly couple behind him. The lady leaned on a purple walker, smiling up at the bent-over man who held matching knit scarves in one hand, the other hand resting on her arm.

"Okay." He stepped aside.

The Oakdale Assisted Living premises needed more parking. Heavy snowflakes plopped from the heavens, splatting the wrapping paper on Logan's three gifts as he tramped around the building to the front door. Between delays at the mall, no parking out front, and now a snowstorm, his scheduled visiting time had dwindled away.

The automatic doors parted and carols filled the lobby. Logan strode to the reception desk, balancing his three large presents. "I'm here to see Lawrence Mitchell."

"He's in the visitors' hall." The woman nodded toward an open door. "You can join him there if you'd like." Seeing Logan's frown, she said, "Or I can get an aide to bring him here."

"Thanks anyway. I'll go." He strode down the corridor to the large room, which held a Christmas tree, a piano, and carolers singing to residents in wheelchairs or sitting beside parked walkers.

Logan spotted his grandfather in the front row, flanked by Caleb and Haley and their mom. So much for his plan to arrive before they showed up. Two rows of wheelchairs were parked behind them. Logan took an empty seat in the back.

A man with a worn Bible stepped to the front. "I'm glad

each one of you is here this afternoon. I'd like to start by reading the Christmas story from Luke chapter two, verses one through five. This is from the New King James Version."

Logan could probably still recite most of the verses from memory. He'd been the narrator enough times at Christmas plays growing up.

"'And it came to pass in those days that a decree went out from Caesar Augustus that all the world should be registered. This census first took place while Quirinius was governing Syria. So all went to be registered, everyone to his own city. Joseph also went up from Galilee, out of the city of Nazareth, into Judea, to the city of David, which is called Bethlehem, because he was of the house and lineage of David, to be registered with Mary, his betrothed wife, who was with child.' This decree inconvenienced people, as it forced them to leave their homes and businesses and to travel—in many cases, a long distance."

Logan felt just like that. Ordered around, inconvenienced, commanded to travel. Well, compelled anyway.

"It was a long and uncomfortable trip, especially for Mary, who was ready to give birth. But God had told her not to be afraid. Joseph received the same message. In Matthew chapter one verse twenty, an angel told him, 'Do not be afraid to take to you Mary your wife.' Within this bold command was embedded a gentle invitation."

Logan slid his fingers along his pants pocket, feeling his wallet with Granddad's note in it. It wasn't an order. It was a gentle invitation.

"Mary and Joseph had to take time away from their daily routine to make this trip. Time away from the things they had planned. From Joseph's carpentry business, his livelihood. Was this trip worth it? Definitely. Because God's plan was fulfilled. Joseph did what God told him to do and went where God led him. The wise men followed God's leading too. So did the shepherds. And they all ended up in the presence of Jesus, God Himself."

Logan couldn't remember when he'd actually felt the presence of God with him.

"Many of you will be giving and receiving gifts during Christmas, and it's great to be generous."

Logan looked at the big-ticket presents he'd set on the floor. Yes, he was very generous.

"God gave the best gift, Christ. And once we receive the gift of salvation, we can be generous with our time. And our love."

Logan was generous with his money. But not so much with his time. And certainly not with his love.

The man closed his Bible. "Let's all sing a Christmas carol before you go back to your rooms."

As the room filled with voices that were far from professionally trained but filled with passion, Logan's presents didn't seem so great after all.

Someone tapped him on the shoulder. He looked up and saw Granddad, holding out his arms. "Think I could get a hug?"

Logan stood and embraced his grandfather.

"I'm mighty glad you came. Any chance you can stick around?" Hope filled his eyes. Haley and Caleb peeked around their great-grandfather with expectant faces. Logan's sister stared at the floor, biting her lip—no doubt dreading the thought of explaining to her children, again, why their uncle was too busy to celebrate Christmas with them.

Logan looked out the window at the pelting snow. He could still drive home in it, if he left soon. Or he could be generous with his time and his love.

"Yeah, Granddad. I can."

Life Application

Have you ever let the Christmas season come and go in all its busyness without really celebrating Christ's greatest gift to us: salvation through His death and resurrection?

Like Logan, perhaps you feel as if you've been issued a series of decrees, directing what you should do, whom you should visit, which social events to attend, maybe even how much to spend on gifts. Since you can't pack all those commitments into your busy schedule or your limited budget, you may be tempted to get by with doing the bare minimum that might be expected by family and friends.

What would happen if we thought of all those stressful Christmas "obligations" as opportunities—invitations to serve others as Christ has served us?

As we celebrate Jesus' birth this year, may we joyously thank Him for fulfilling what He came to earth to do—giving

His very life as the perfect gift for sinners. "The gift of God is eternal life in Christ Jesus our Lord" (Romans 6:23 NKJV).

About the Author

Barbara Curtis lives in Connecticut with her family (and two cats and a dog). She loves editing and writing, especially fiction, finding it a way to fulfill Psalm 34:3: "Oh, magnify the Lord with me, and let us exalt His name together" (NKJV).

15

Rainbow-Colored Promises

by Kelly Wilson Mize

The familiar sensation of grief flooded Faith's heart once again. Over the past year, she couldn't remember a time when the reality of it hadn't consumed her. In her younger life, she'd enjoyed many happy days and carefree times. But the intermittent "waves of doom," as she had come to think of them, brought an unwelcome darkness that seemed to have become a part of her very soul. The most recent wave had lasted way too long, and its evil power over her, whether real or imagined, grew with each passing day.

Light had always been soothing therapy for the dark times. Faith had learned early on that light could defeat the darkness, laugh in its face. The healing properties of light came in many forms: simple sunshine, a lamp turned on in a dark house, candles on a birthday cake. In the winter, Christmas lights brought warmth and joy to a cold, vulnerable soul.

Faith had come to love colored lights as a little girl. Her

family never had money for extravagant holiday decorations, but Faith was sure that their Christmas tree was prettier and brighter than any of her friends' trees or even those at the mall. Her parents worked hard every year to make it beautiful. The lights were multicolored magic.

Amid the sparkle and shine, Faith's family never forgot the true meaning of the season. On Christmas Eve, they paused to quietly reflect on the baby King, born in a manger to an ordinary family, who brought light into a dark world. Her father always used Christmas lights to represent Jesus as the Light of the World. "The light shines in the darkness, and the darkness has not overcome it," he would say, quoting John 1:5. Faith and her siblings could recite parts of John 1, their father's favorite Scripture passage, from the time they could talk, never realizing that there would be times in their lives when the darkness would be so difficult to overcome.

Today, even Christmas lights couldn't cheer Faith. The twinkling beacons actually seemed to mock her. Everyone around her appeared blissfully filled with the Christmas spirit: her family, friends, strangers in the grocery store, TV personalities, and everyone in the world of social media.

But not Faith. Not this year.

The day after Thanksgiving last November, a stoic doctor had explained the cruel diagnosis and its lightning-fast effects. Behind his desk, medical diplomas and awards hung on the wall, the glass that covered them reflecting the lights of a glistening Christmas tree. Eighteen days later, her father was gone.

How ironic that the sight of Christmas lights, which had always been a source of joy to Faith, now triggered that horrible memory. A beautiful tradition ruined forever.

After her dad's death, Faith had tried to carry on. She bought Christmas presents for her children but didn't have the strength to decorate the house, not even for them. Her husband had put up the tree, but Faith avoided the sight of it. And she'd pleaded that the multicolored lights they'd always used be replaced with simple white ones.

This year, things would be different. She had to be strong for her children. The painful memory of their grandfather's death didn't prevent them from buzzing with excitement at the prospect of a new Christmas season.

December 15 taunted Faith from the Advent calendar on the wall. Turning from the festive reminder, she stared at the artificial tree waiting to be clothed. With a sigh, she plodded up the stairs to drag buckets, baskets, and boxes of snowmen, wreaths, garland, bows, and lights from the attic.

The first box she opened was the one with the lights. The modern, simple, elegant white ones she'd begged her husband to get last year.

"Mom?" Eight-year-old Holly tapped her shoulder. "Can we use the colored lights this time?"

Faith swallowed back a sob. How could she explain to her daughter that multicolored lights were heart-breaking reminders of her father's passing? And yet … how could she deprive her children of the sense of magic that those colorful lights had brought to her at their age?

"That sounds like a great idea," she answered weakly. "But let's go to the store and see if we can find some new ones."

Holly squealed and clapped her little hands with delight. "Daddy will be so surprised when he comes home from work and sees our new lights!"

Indeed.

Two hours later, Faith and her children returned with two boxes of multicolored Christmas lights, some new silver tinsel, and a box of tissue, because Faith knew she would probably need it.

Six-year-old Timothy opened the first box of new lights so eagerly the cardboard ripped. "Look! Every string has red, yellow, green, and blue lights. That's almost all the colors of the rainbow!"

Faith smiled at her son's enthusiasm. As they strung the lights, she remembered the story of Noah's ark. After the devastating deluge, God sent a rainbow as a sign to remind His people that He would never again destroy the earth with a flood. The Bible was filled with promises from God. If only Faith could truly believe them once again.

Feeling the need for a break, she excused herself to the kitchen. "I've got my own flood to deal with," she moaned under her breath. She needed to stop feeling sorry for herself, but she didn't know how. *God, please heal my grief and sorrow.*

After using up a few of the tissues she'd just purchased, Faith returned to the living room. The children had strung the new lights haphazardly around the tree. The sight of their imperfect handiwork brought tears of a different kind to Faith's eyes. Holly was right. The multicolored lights were prettier than the white ones. A lot prettier.

The enchanting vision brought an unexpected sense of peace to Faith's heart. Even though the glow of the colored lights still reminded her of the sad events of last year, they also brought back memories of the happy days of her childhood, the love of her father, and the joy of Christmas. The colors of the rainbow represented a sign of hope.

For the first time in a long time, Faith felt like everything might be okay after all. In that moment, she could almost hear her father recite the familiar words of John 1:5: "The light shines in the darkness, and the darkness has not overcome it."

In her heart, Faith knew that the "flooding wave of doom" would not overwhelm her again. Instead, every time she looked at the lights on her lovely Christmas tree, or any of the other beautiful lights in the world, she would remember the truth of God's promises. And know that they were meant for her.

Life Application

Do you feel void of hope in this joyous season? You're not alone. We all have moments of sadness, and those feelings can be magnified when the people around us seem so happy and fulfilled. The good news is that God can use anything—even Christmas lights—to gently remind us of His love.

The Bible is filled with promises that God makes to His people for their good. Even though His timing often isn't what we would choose, we can rest assured that His will is best, no matter what the circumstances are. Therefore, there is always reason to hope.

So take heart. The Light has overcome the world!

About the Author

Kelly Wilson Mize is a wife, mother, educator, and free-lance writer living in Huntsville, Alabama. Her work has appeared in a variety of books, magazines, newspapers, and online publications for children and adults. Credits include stories, articles, devotions, and curriculum for LifeWay Christian Resources, Group Publishing, Adams Media, and Focus on the Family. Kelly recently became a member of The Christian PEN. She has a master's degree in elementary education and currently serves as a librarian at Westminster Christian Academy.

Doubting Thomas

by Nanette Thorsen-Snipes

Divorced. The word echoed in Tommie Jo's brain. The decision had been hard to make, but after her husband's last affair, it was easier. The spring and summer following the divorce were tough, but somehow, with God's help, she'd made it through.

Summer slid crazily into fall. Soon it was the Christmas season, and even though she worked hard, she had no extra money. A tension headache started in the back of her head as she contemplated what she and her daughter would have to give up for even a small Christmas.

Ten-year-old Hallie stood at their townhome's picture window, mesmerized by the blinking lights on the tree across the street. "Mama, that tree is so pretty. When are we going to get one?"

"I don't know, honey." Tommie Jo's thoughts bounced around in her throbbing head. She'd get paid a couple of days before Christmas. Maybe then they could get a tree and a few presents.

"I want a tree like the one we saw in that store the other day, with all the fancy brown balls with powder-blue polka dots on them." Hallie's green eyes brightened at the prospect. "Please, Mama?"

"I don't think we can afford a tree like that, or even new ornaments." Tommie Jo looked down at her hands, wondering where she could find a cheap tree.

The days zoomed by as Tommie Jo worked, inputting patients' names and addresses into the computer. Occasionally she answered phones and made appointments. It was monotonous work, but it brought in a paycheck.

And yet, here it was, two days before Christmas, and she barely had enough money for a couple of presents.

Tommie Jo missed the luxury of being able to buy a pile of nice gifts for Hallie—although she didn't miss the arguments she got from her ex over every purchase. She also felt nostalgic for the white Christmases she'd grown up with. The streets here in south Georgia rarely got enough flakes to make a snowball, much less go sledding. And it never snowed on Christmas Eve.

When she stopped by the babysitter's house to pick up Hallie, she asked, "Could I pay you when my next check comes in?"

"Of course." Her longtime sitter used age-spotted fingers to push a few wisps of gray hair away from her sagging jawline. "Are you having money problems, child?" she asked softly.

Unable to come up with an appropriate answer, Tommie Jo helped Hallie get into her coat.

"You know, prayer never hurt anyone."

Yeah, right. God wasn't interested in her prayers. He was too busy taking care of the really big things, like wars and terminal diseases. She didn't want to bother God with a silly request for a Christmas tree.

"Thanks for watching Hallie, Mrs. Pearson." Tommie Jo grabbed her daughter's hand and hurried to her car.

As she backed out of the driveway, she noticed something glistening in the ditch. She stopped to get a better look. The small artificial tree had certainly been through a number of Christmases.

"Look, Hallie, a tree!"

"But, Mama, it's old."

"That doesn't matter. After we put our lights and ornaments on it, it'll be beautiful." Tommie Jo jumped out of the car and stuffed it into the trunk. *All we need now is some snow.* When she climbed back in, she noticed Hallie's sour expression.

"It might look okay if we had some of those fancy brown balls with powder-blue polka dots all over them."

"I know, sweetie, but we can't afford them."

Silence rode with them the rest of the way home.

After cleaning their townhouse, Tommie Jo brought down the boxes of ornaments and lights. She straightened out a few limbs to make the tree look a little fuller, wrapped two strands of lights around it, then plugged them in. "Isn't it amazing?"

Hallie crossed her arms over her chest. "It's still an old tree."

Tommie Jo headed to the kitchen to make hot chocolate with marshmallows. When she returned to the living room, she found her daughter looking out the window, her face beaming.

"Look, Mama. It's snowing!"

Warming her hands on the mug, Tommie Jo watched the wet snowflakes fall. Soon the ground in front of the townhouse wore a pristine winter coat.

God had answered her two unspoken prayers!

Forgive me, Father, for doubting You.

With fresh enthusiasm, she returned to sorting through their old ornaments. Someday she'd be able to buy new ones. Fancy brown ones with powder-blue polka dots would be nice.

Hallie rummaged through the beat-up ornament box, pulling out red and blue balls. Together they placed them on the tree, then added some gold and green ones, spacing them out so there was plenty of room for the timeworn family ornaments in the second box.

Hallie pulled out the first one. "Look, Mama! It's a rattle with my name on it."

"I got that for you not long after you were born." Tommie Jo placed the ornament near the top of the tree. "Do you know what it reminds me of?"

"What?" Hallie's eyes sparkled.

"Another baby, who was born a long time ago—Jesus. He was special too. An angel appeared to His mother, Mary, to announce His birth. After He arrived, I'm sure she sang praises to God while she cradled Jesus in her arms."

Hallie reached into the pile of ornaments and pulled out a lopsided Styrofoam cup wrapped in tin foil, meant to resemble a bell.

"Your dad made that with you."

"I know. We had a lot of fun making it."

Tommie Jo found a wire hook, threaded it through the red yarn attached to the bell, and hung it on the tree. Then she pulled out a large, hand-painted ball that sported a bright star shining down on a stable. "This reminds me of the star of Bethlehem. I can almost see the three wise men staring at it in amazement and then following it to the manger."

She pulled out the last ornament in the box. "Your grandma and grandpa gave me this angel tree topper many years ago." She fingered its golden wings, then placed it at the top. "It reminds me of the angel that appeared to the shepherds, proclaiming the birth of Jesus."

Tommie Jo and Hallie stood back to admire the tree. "Mama! The story of Jesus is mixed up with our ornaments!"

Tears fogged Tommie Jo's vision. "Jesus always gets mixed up in our lives, doesn't He?"

Thank You, Father, for knowing my heart and granting my requests, even though I didn't believe enough to ask for them. Forgive me for being such a doubting Thomas.

"We didn't need a tree dressed up in fancy polka-dotted balls, did we, Mama? All we needed was our family memories." Hallie sat on the carpeted floor and took the last sip of her hot chocolate, the blinking lights from the tree reflecting in her eyes.

Tommie Jo sat down beside her. "After supper tonight, let's read the Christmas story."

Life Application

Prayer is communication with God, our Father, through Jesus Christ, our mediator. God loves and cares for each of us, and when we commune with Him, our prayers rise up as a sweet fragrance.

First Peter 5:7 encourages us to cast our cares and anxieties on God because He cares for us—not just the big concerns, but all of them. God cares about every little thing that happens to us. And He hears our prayers even before they leave our lips. Isaiah 65:24 says, "Before they call I will answer; while they are still speaking I will hear."

About the Author

Nanette Thorsen-Snipes has published more than five hundred articles, columns, and reprints in more than forty publications and more than fifty-five compilation books, including stories in three *Guideposts* anthologies in the Miracles series, in *The New Women's Devotional Bible*, and in *Grace Givers.* She lives in north Georgia with her husband, Jim. They have four grown children and eight grandchildren. Find her at FaithWorksEditorial.com.

17

A Family to Hope For

by Marilyn Hilton

Tony Prescott squinted against the glare of headlights reflected on the rain-slicked road as he drove home from his last contract job before Christmas.

"Should have left earlier," he chided himself. But the homeowner's kitchen needed final touch-ups, and Tony had wanted to finish today. Preserving his reputation wasn't the only reason he worked late every day. He had no family to go home to.

"Andrew, would you please stir the sauce for me?" Caroline Lawson carried three sets of silverware to the dining table decorated for Christmas. For a moment, she watched her little man, already six, stirring the simmering pasta sauce. Every Christmas Eve since their marriage, Doug had made spaghetti and meatballs, garlic bread, and salad for dinner. Now, two Christmases had passed since his unexpected death, and Caroline had continued the tradition, hoping to make it her children's as well.

"Kaylee," she called up the stairs, "dinnertime."

After everyone was seated at the table, they bowed their heads for grace.

"Dear God," Caroline said, "thank You for this food. Thank You for our family. Thank You for Your Son, whose birth we celebrate tonight."

"And thanks for Mom," Kaylee said.

"And please send us a daddy," Andrew added.

A daddy? Caroline's eyes stung behind her closed lids. Neither child had expressed a desire for a new father. But lately, she had been wishing there might be someone she could fall in love with and who would feel the same for her, who would love her children and share the everyday worries and joys.

"Thank You, Lord. Amen." She gave each hand a little squeeze.

Andrew poked at the meatball on his plate. "Mom, do you think He will?"

"Will what, honey?"

"Send us a new dad." Andrew popped the meatball into his mouth, ringing his lips with sauce.

Caroline wiped her son's face with her napkin. "Maybe someday. But only if it's what God wants for us."

"Then let's keep praying," Kaylee said, winding a forkful of pasta.

Christmas Eve used to be a magical night, Tony thought as he peered through the windshield wipers at house after house decorated for Christmas. In the past, he'd ushered at Christmas Eve services or sung in the choir, feeling the presence of God and the breathless expectation of Jesus' birth. But after years of living alone and focusing on his contracting business, that magic had faded, leaving him empty.

As he maneuvered his pickup through the rain, Tony thought about the people inside the homes he passed. Kids listening for Santa, parents wrapping gifts, relatives arriving and settling in, families preparing to sing and worship together in church and light the final Advent candle.

Tony recalled the sense of peace and expectation he'd always felt seeing the Christ candle glow in the dim sanctuary, its flame dancing.

Now, with rain beating on the roof, he prayed for the first time in months. "Lord, forgive me for leaving You. Please draw me close again."

The rain became a downpour. The wipers, already at full speed, couldn't keep the windshield clear. Tony eased up on the accelerator and concentrated on the road ahead.

Something darted across the street in front of him. Tony gripped the steering wheel and swerved right. With a screech of tires and a sickening thud, the truck leaped up the curb and plunged into a fence.

The airbag deployed, hitting Tony full in the face. The acrid smell of powder filled his nostrils.

In the glow of his headlights, he inspected the fence he'd hit. A shattered post lay on the lawn behind it, and the railings were askew. Repairs could cost a few hundred dollars. Fortunately, the impact had stopped the truck from going farther onto the lawn.

Tony got out and checked the front of his truck. The post had pushed in the grille. He'd have to get his mechanic to check the engine. But would the pickup make it to the shop? Even if it could, when would he take it in? The shop would be closed for the holidays. And his next job started two days after Christmas.

First things first. He had to tell the people who owned the house behind this fence what happened, apologize, and pay them for the repairs.

He limped up the sidewalk. With colorful lights framing the roofline and a wreath at the front door, it looked like the perfect Christmas house. Through the picture window, he saw a woman and two children eating and laughing. A festive tree glittered behind them.

The scene tugged at Tony's heart. He hated having to deliver bad news, especially on Christmas Eve.

He ran a hand through his hair, then rang the bell. The woman he'd seen through the window opened the door. Her expression radiated warmth and kindness. *That won't last long.*

The man standing at Caroline's door looked like he'd been punched in the face. He also looked forlorn.

"Can I help you?"

"My name is Tony Prescott. My pickup skidded out there, and your fence stopped me."

Caroline's heart thudded. "Are you hurt?"

He touched his cheek. "The airbag got me. But I'm fine. Unfortunately, your fence isn't. I want to apologize and pay for the damages."

"Please come in." She opened the door wider. "I'm Caroline." For a moment, she thought she should be more cautious about letting a stranger into the house. But a sense of peace told her this man was trustworthy. "Do you need to call anyone?"

"I'd like to call my mechanic before he closes." He pulled his cell phone from his pocket.

"Save your battery. You're welcome to use our phone."

As she led Tony to the kitchen, Andrew and Kaylee called out, "Merry Christmas!"

"Merry Christmas," Tony answered. The sight of the two youngsters stirred a desire in his heart for a family like this, with a wife who was kind to strangers and children who were sweet and well mannered. The man of this house was one lucky guy.

He called his mechanic, but a holiday greeting sent him to voicemail.

"Any luck?" Caroline asked when he hung up.

"Afraid not. He'll be closed till after New Year's Day."

"My brother's shop will be open the day after tomorrow." She opened a drawer and handed him a business card.

When Tony looked at it, he recognized the name. "Don't two guys own this shop?"

"Yes." Caroline looked away. "My brother took it over after my husband died a few years ago."

"I'm sorry." Tony felt a rush of sympathy for her.

"It gets harder this time of year, but we're fine." Her warm smile returned.

"Thanks for letting me use your phone. And please let me know how much the fence costs to fix." He handed her his business card.

As he turned toward the door, the children smiled and waved their forks.

"Do you think that was him?" he heard the boy whisper.

"Who?" Caroline asked.

"The man we prayed for."

As Caroline walked him to the door, her cheeks were scarlet. Tony wondered why.

"I'm really sorry for wrecking your fence."

She smiled. "Don't worry about it. Most everything can be made new again."

As he returned to his truck, he thought about her words. Yes, most everything could be made new again. A fence. An engine. Even a heart.

Life Application

For some people, Christmas is not a joyful time. We struggle with financial, relationship, or personal issues. We're grieving past losses. We worry about the future. We struggle with unrealized expectations. For so long we've hoped for a spouse, or a cure, or enough funds to cover our bills. Finally, we give up hoping.

Paul wrote, "Hope that is seen is no hope at all. Who hopes for what they already have? But if we hope for what we do not yet have, we wait for it patiently" (Romans 8:24–25).

Christmas is the season of hope, as we celebrate the birth of Jesus, the Light of the World. Like waiting for the dawn after a long, dark night and seeing the sky grow rosy and then brilliant, we can be sure that God will fulfill His promises to those who seek, wait, and hope.

About the Author

Marilyn Hilton is the author of *Full Cicada Moon, Found Things, It's All About Dad & Me,* and *The Christian Girl's Guide to Your Mom.* She has also published numerous articles, devotions, and award-winning short stories and poems. She enjoys leading Bible studies for adults and teens. Visit Marilyn at marilynhilton.com.

18

Home for Christmas

by Esther G. Seim

Gray. That's the only color here in the dingy halls of Applewood Group Home. Gray walls. Blue-gray blankets on the beds. Gray metal furniture. Gray bars over the windows to keep rebels from running away. One time, a rainbow formed over the group home. That's about the closest thing to color that's ever been near this place.

I'm sick of gray.

"Addisyn, the bus is here."

I look up and see Mrs. Fournier at the door of my room. "Yes, ma'am."

She frowns at me. "What in the world happened to your hair?"

I rake my fingers through my wild black curls. "I took the braids out. They made me look like a six-year-old."

Mrs. Fournier exhales. "Whatever. Just get going."

"Yes, ma'am." I grab my backpack off my lower bunk and

dash out the bedroom door and into the hallway. I hate school even more than the color gray. It's not that I'm a bad student. I'm in the top 10 percent of my class in every subject except PE. But my smarts don't make me very popular. So I have no friends.

"Forgetting something?" Mrs. Fournier walks toward me, holding up a picture I was assigned to paint for my school choir's field trip to a nursing home after lunch today.

I take it. "Thanks." I push through the double doors and join the other groupies in the frigid air as they wait in line to board the bus. I shiver through my thin coat. December is here, and Christmas is right around the corner. Any day now, Mrs. Fournier will go up into the attic and bring down the dusty artificial tree. Only half of its lights work, but she never notices. On Christmas Eve, the Rotary Club will bring presents. Matchbox cars for the boys and dolls for the girls. Problem is, I'm thirteen. I don't play with dolls anymore.

❄

"Jingle bells, jingle bells." Along with the other kids from my school choir, I belt out the popular holiday carol. Now, I can't carry a tune in a bucket, but most of the other kids can't either. The old folks don't seem to care. They watch us with intent smiles ... well, except for a snoozing gentleman sitting at the front. His snores seem to punctuate each note of the song.

We finish, and our teacher stands. "Ladies and gentlemen, that concludes our performance."

The audience applauds.

The sleeping gentleman awakes with a start. "Is it over?"

Our teacher clears her throat. "The children have made holiday pictures for each of you." She turns to us. "Go pass them out."

I kneel, unzip my backpack, and pull out my picture—a painting of a Christmas tree. I scan the crowd, searching for the perfect recipient.

My gaze lands on a lady in a wheelchair. Her white curls remind me of fresh snow. I walk toward her and hand her my picture. "Happy holidays."

She gives me a glowing smile. "Thank you, dearie. Won't you sit down?"

Nervous, I perch on the empty folding chair next to her.

"What's your name, hon?"

"Addisyn."

"I'm Millie." She holds up my picture. "Did you paint this?"

"Yeah."

"You're a wonderful artist." Miss Millie points to the yellow star at the top. "Do you know what this stands for?"

It's a star. I didn't know it was supposed to mean something.

"Many years ago, God used a star to announce His Son's birth into this world. That baby's name was Jesus. Have your parents ever told you about Jesus?"

A lump forms in my throat. "I live in a group home." I look into her eyes, waiting for her reaction. But she doesn't freak out like people usually do. She acts as if she didn't even hear me. I subtly check for a hearing aid.

"When Jesus grew into a man, He taught folks about God's kingdom and healed the sick. But many people didn't like Jesus. Some had Him killed."

I gasp. "How could anybody get away with killing God's Son?"

Miss Millie's eyes get misty. "Jesus let them. He was willing to go through all that pain … for me and for you."

I raise an eyebrow. "How can a man's death help me?"

"Because through it, you can live forever."

Now I'm more confused than ever. So I change the subject. "Do you live here?"

"No. I'm recovering from a knee-replacement surgery." She motions to her bandaged leg, propped up on the chair in front of her.

"Then you'll go home to your family?"

"My Bernie died many years ago, and we didn't have any children."

"Then you're like me." The words slip out before I realize I'm thinking aloud.

"How so?"

My cheeks heat up. "You've got no family."

Miss Millie and I talk for at least another half hour. She asks me about school, my hobbies. I can't remember the last time an adult has taken so much interest in me.

A nurse comes up behind Miss Millie, interrupting our conversation. "It's time for your doctor's appointment, Ms. Vincent."

"Thank you, Cecelia." Miss Millie pulls a well-worn black

book out of the purse on her lap. "I want you to have this, Addisyn. Read the book of John first."

I take the gift, and the nurse wheels Miss Millie away.

I open the front cover. On the first page is an inscription:

To my lovely wife, Mildred.

May this blessed book guide you through life and comfort you in your darkest hours. Someday I hope this Bible will be passed on to our children.

Love, Bernie

Christmas 1960

This book must be very dear to Miss Millie. I want to run and give it back to her, but I know she gave it to me for a reason. I clutch it to my chest. A foreign sensation creeps into my heart. I think it might be … hope.

"Get your feet off my dashboard."

I look up from my Bible. "Sorry, Mrs. Fournier." I take down my feet and stare at the street before us. Two days ago, I was assigned a new foster home. Today I'm going to meet my next temporary parents. I'm not new to this process—but it still unnerves me.

"And put your book away. We're almost there." Mrs. Fournier reminds me of a little kid in need of a nap.

I place my Bible inside my bag, bookmarking the page I'm on. I finished John two days ago, then decided to start at the beginning, in Genesis.

Mrs. Fournier turns into a neighborhood. The picturesque two-story homes have brick architecture and snow-covered lawns.

At the end of a cul-de-sac, Mrs. Fournier pulls into the driveway of the prettiest house on the block. Multicolored Christmas lights line the roof—the large kind, like old people have.

Across the street, a little boy and a girl about my age make a snowman in their front yard. The girl smiles and waves to us—almost as if she knows who I am. I wave back, feeling bashful. Yet also guardedly hopeful.

Mrs. Fournier stops the engine and we get out. I grab my bag and we walk up a path toward the house.

My heart beats like a bongo drum. What will these people be like? Nice? Mean? Maybe they're a rich couple who want to make me their maid.

Mrs. Fournier rings the bell. I hold my breath until the door opens. A familiar face greets me.

"Miss Millie?"

She steps out onto the porch and envelops me in a big hug. "I'm so glad you're finally here. I've been searching for you at all the group homes in the area."

I step back, my mind spinning. "You have?"

She extends her hand toward her open door. "I've got cinnamon tea and gingerbread cookies in the kitchen."

"None for me, thanks," Mrs. Fournier says. "I've got to run. But I'll be back in two hours. You listen to Ms. Vincent, Addisyn, you hear?"

"Can't I just move in here now?" I blurt out.

"Addisyn!" Mrs. Fournier purses her lips. "Mind your manners."

Miss Millie puts up her hand. "It's quite all right. Addisyn and I are already acquainted. I wouldn't mind skipping all the visitations. If that's acceptable with you."

Mrs. Fournier looks from Miss Millie to me as if she doesn't know what to say. "My assistant will come by tomorrow with the remaining paperwork and Addisyn's belongings." She turns on her heel and walks toward her car.

I look up at Miss Millie, then back at the grumpy old woman's retreating figure. "Mrs. Fournier?"

She stops and turns toward me, her ever-present impatient scowl more pronounced than ever. "What?"

I gulp. "M-merry Christmas. Jesus loves you."

For the first time, I see something close to a smile soften the corners of her mouth. "Thanks." She gets in her car.

Miss Millie lays a hand on my shoulder. "You've been reading that Bible, haven't you?"

"Every chance I get!" I follow her inside. The living room is warm and cozy. A Christmas tree about my height sits in the corner, and two red stockings are hung by a crackling fireplace. One of the stockings bears my name in glittering gold letters. On the mantel is a framed painting—my Christmas tree!

"Welcome home, Addisyn."

As I stare at a beautiful ceramic nativity set on the coffee table, I realize something. Jesus has come home too … in my heart.

Life Application

Orphans like Addisyn are everywhere. Even if they have earthly parents, they lack a heavenly Father. These spiritual orphans need the greatest gift of all: the Savior who came to earth as a little baby to offer Himself as a sacrifice for their sins.

You can be the messenger God uses to tell others about this irreplaceable and priceless gift, which keeps giving for all eternity. Sometimes all it takes is a simple present. Or a few moments of your time.

About the Author

Esther Seim is seventeen years old and has been writing fiction since she was nine. She especially enjoys writing for children and teens. She also writes Christian book reviews for *Clash Entertainment* and has started *Clash 4 Kids* (clash4kids.com). When she's not writing, she enjoys life in Arkansas as a homeschool student and ballet teacher.

19

All I Want for Christmas

by Glenda Joy Race

Lori awoke to the sound of Korean voices singing what sounded like "Victory in Jesus." Normally she loved singing. But not at five o'clock in the morning.

She groaned. "All I want for Christmas is to sleep till noon." Lori laughed. As an English teacher living in South Korea, that wish wasn't likely to come true.

The congregation switched to singing a rousing rendition of "I'll Fly Away." No use even trying to go back to sleep now.

Gathering together to praise God at five a.m. wasn't a bad thing—if they did it in the mountains. But singing right next door to her home made Lori feel … inconvenienced.

After getting dressed, she opened her English Bible and turned the pages to the passage for that day. She read about the tower of Babel. As mankind attempted to build a monument to reach the heavens, God was displeased. He confused their speech so they couldn't proceed with their construction. Humankind dispersed.

Lori thought about the language barrier she'd experienced here. When she first arrived, she couldn't even order at a fast-food restaurant. Yet that very difficulty had given her the opportunity to teach here.

After five minutes of going through her list of prayer requests, Lori decided to face the day … at five-thirty.

Her coworkers had all gone home to the United States or Canada for Christmas, but Lori had decided to stay in Seoul, wanting to save money. As she sat alone in her empty living area, sipping boiled barley tea, she began to question that decision.

Her parents had arranged to make a video recording of friends and family, hoping that would stave off the homesickness. Each passing day made her more eager for the package to arrive.

The phone rang. Lori's heart skipped when she heard her mother's voice.

"I'm afraid I have some bad news."

She sat in a cane chair and braced herself.

"Your Uncle David passed away."

Waves of regret tsunamied over Lori's heart. She wanted to reach through the line and give her mom a hug. Tears flowed down her face and shame burned her cheeks. "Maybe I can come home for the funeral."

"Actually, the service was last weekend."

Lori choked back a sob. "I need to get going if I want anything for breakfast besides my roommate's leftover kimchi."

"Keem-what?"

"It's a spicy pickled cabbage."

"Sounds … healthy."

"Yeah." But a poor substitute for her mother's homemade gingerbread.

After a breakfast of Asian pear juice, brown eggs, and bread, Lori felt ready to start her day.

As she walked to the school, she thought about her students. The class was a mixture of Korean, American, and international children. Most had at least one English-speaking parent. Lori's responsibility was teaching fifteen fourth graders. Her group was small compared to most classrooms, but the need for individual attention and classroom discipline kept her constantly busy.

Mi-wah, who'd picked Miriam for her English name, was the spelling-test perfectionist. Timothy's parents were Americans who taught English at a local college. Then there were the missionary-kid twins, Stephen and Joy. Stephen was already telling his peers about Jesus. Joy was the quiet one, except when it was time to sing.

Lori loved all of her students. They gave her a sense of fulfillment she hadn't found substitute teaching in the United States.

As she organized her books for the day, she found herself worrying about Uncle David's widow, Aunt Nancy, and her cousins, Brad and Naomi. They were a close-knit family who had devotions together every morning. Would they continue in their faithfulness?

Mi-wah came in and placed a pencil on Lori's desk. "Morning, Teacher."

On the first day of school, Lori had tried to instruct her students to call her Miss Ross. But they kept saying, "Miss Loss," so Lori allowed them to refer to her as Teacher. In South Korea it was a term of respect.

The children all stood and sang the United States and South Korean national anthems. Then they wrote their journal entries for the day. After that, it was time for free-time reading. Next, Lori introduced vocabulary for a selection from *Pilgrim's Progress*. They all enjoyed the reading and the lively discussion that followed. For math, the students studied liters and gallons.

When the children went outside for lunch and recess, Lori checked her e-mail, then went to the office, which was little more than the secretary's desk.

"A package came for you." Hanna handed her a small box.

Lori squealed. "It's a video recording from my parents."

"Maybe you could show it in your class this afternoon."

"It isn't educational."

"Sure, it is." Mr. Solomon, the principal, stepped into the room. "Your students can join the fifth and sixth graders for American Cultures."

Lori was so overjoyed she couldn't finish her sandwich.

After lunch, the desks were shoved to the outer edges of the big room, and the three classes of students sat on the floor to watch the movie.

It started with a display of the colorful leaves on the mountains in northeastern Pennsylvania. Next was Lori's family on the steps of their church. Both of her younger brothers waved excitedly. Uncle David, Aunt Nancy, and their children sent her greetings.

Lori's eyes stung and her throat closed up. She hadn't realized how homesick she'd been until she saw her loved ones back home—including one she would not see again this side of heaven.

The next scene showed the family gathered for Sunday dinner. After the group video ended, Lori's mom announced that the church had collected a love offering so she could visit Lori in South Korea.

As tears streaked down her face, the children clapped.

That evening, Lori called home to thank her mother for the video. They started planning for her visit. They would go to shopping centers and markets, restaurants, and the Everland theme park. And attend the Korean church's Sunday service.

"Please bring lots of cinnamon, marshmallows, and oatmeal."

Mom laughed at her list of "American" foods that could not be found in the Korean market.

"Oh, and my favorite zucchini bars." Lori looked forward to fooling her Korean friends with the lemon, sugar, and cinnamon in those treats that made the zucchini taste like apple pie.

The next morning, Lori woke before the five o'clock Christmas carols started. As the young people sang "Silent

Night" and wished one another *jilgohun Christmas bonoseyo,* Lori sank to her knees in grateful prayer.

Life Application

Many people are isolated at Christmas, separated from those they love by geographical distance, emotional issues, or death. Even if you're directly in the center of God's will, you may feel homesick for the people and things you've left behind.

If you feel alone this Christmas, think about the people God has brought into your life. Connect with them, even if only by phone, text, or e-mail. Or perhaps a video recording. Let them know how much you appreciate their impact on your life.

About the Author

Glenda Joy Race, a teacher and writer from northeastern Pennsylvania, teaches basic writing skills and fundamentals of writing at Luzerne County Community College. She has written poetry, devotionals, and nonfiction articles. Her writing has been featured in children's magazines. She also edits *Poetry on Recovery*, an annual publication dedicated to mental health awareness month.

20

A White Christmas with You

by Rachael Landis

These ugly walls are closing in on me.

The harsh hospital lights illuminated flaking white paint on the walls. The fifty-year-old building was falling apart. But instead of constructing a new one, the city officials contented themselves with additions. Nicole bet this place would still be under construction when she retired.

She was on her last leg of a twelve-hour shift. The food in the vending machine was starting to look appealing. Time to get out of here.

Two days before Christmas and the emergency room was bustling, as usual. Nurses scurried and doctors dashed from patient to patient.

"Nicole!" someone shouted.

She turned and saw Dave, a newly hired doctor who

constantly spoke of bringing change to the department. “Calming the chaos from within” was one of his favorite catchphrases.

“I need you to check on the patient in room 32. Here’s the chart. I know it’s your last hour, but remember … a smile does more than brighten a room; it lightens a heart. Go light up that room.”

It took all her willpower to refrain from asking where the lighter fluid was. He would probably say it was inside her.

She wasn’t usually this Scrooge-like, she mused on her way to the room. This holiday season just seemed to push her past the brink of “deck the halls” to burning them down.

Nothing dramatic had changed from the last year until now. But a gradual realization had dawned on her that all the lights and presents, the good feelings and sappy carols, didn’t change anything for her. Nicole loved her family, but her siblings all had kids of their own, some even grandchildren. All she had was herself. And she was tired of being alone.

Swiping room 32’s curtain back, she prayed for a little extra patience and entered. The elderly lady reached out to her.

“Good evening, Mrs. Anderson,” she said, flipping through the chart. “My name is Nicole, and I’m going to be your nurse for tonight. Looks like you are here for chest pains. The doctor will be in as soon as he can. In the meantime, I’ll check your vitals.”

Listening through the stethoscope, Nicole heard the old woman’s heart beat wildly.

"Is this the end?" she asked, her voice frail. "I know I'm old, but just before Christmas ...?"

"No, Mrs. Anderson—"

"Please call me Grace."

"All right. Grace, your heart rate is higher than normal, but we won't know anything for sure until the doctor comes."

"I need to call my husband." Panic deepened the creases in her forehead, and her sky-blue eyes swelled with tears. "Timmy needs to know."

"The nurse who checked you in probably called him already. But if you'd like, I can check to make sure." Nicole gritted her teeth. She hated adding one more thing to her to-do list.

"Oh, thank you. And what's your name, dear?"

Nicole grimaced. She always introduced herself the moment she entered a room. A glance at the woman's chart told her dementia was setting in. That explained it. "I'm Nicole."

Grace fluffed her matted white curls. "Timmy is going to love my new hairdo. He likes it when I change things up." Her eyes glazed over, and for a moment Nicole felt intrusive, as if she were party to a private moment where she wasn't invited. She seized her chance and slipped from the room.

When she returned at the end of her shift, Nicole heard Grace talking to herself.

"Not a creature was stirring, not even a mouse."

Nicole recognized the poem but wasn't sure why the woman was saying it. Or to whom.

"How are you feeling, Grace?"

"Oh, I've had better days. But you know, I can't be ungrateful. The Lord gives me grace for even the hard ones."

Nicole propped the elderly lady up with a pillow. The starched hospital sheets fell limp over her skinny frame.

"My, my, look at all these wrinkles." Grace held up her arm and pinched the extra skin.

"Why, you must not be a day over sixty," Nicole said in an attempt to lighten the mood.

"When will Timmy be here?"

"Soon, I'm sure." Nicole chided herself for not taking the time to check. "How long have you been married?" she asked, hoping to distract Grace.

"Not more than a decade. But when you're as old as we are, each moment feels like an eternity. Then again, forever doesn't last, at least not on this earth. My body is going to give up someday. Thank God, the Lord will be there when it does."

Nicole wasn't so sure about that. She believed in God, but after years of silence from Him, she had trouble believing He actually cared about the little things.

"Maybe today is that day." Grace's frail image took on the likeness of a child. Her eyes searched Nicole's, clearly looking for peace and assurance. But Nicole could give neither of those.

The next few minutes stretched on in silence as she searched her mind for something to say or do.

"Will you sing with me, dear?"

Sing? Nicole didn't sing. Not well, anyway.

Grace started in on "I'm Dreaming of a White Christmas." In the middle of the second verse, her voice cracked and the volume lowered to a whisper. Nicole leaned in close and picked up the tune. They sang in hushed voices. And in the still of that room, all the noise from the rest of the hospital grew distant.

Finishing the last phrase, Grace closed her eyes, clearly stuck in memories of a time when a white Christmas wasn't hospital walls but snow.

"I am dreaming of a white Christmas with you, Timmy," she said. "Just like the ones we used to have."

Grace whimpered, Nicole guessed from another shot of chest pain. When she opened her eyes, they were blurry with pain and confusion. "What's your name, dearie?"

Nicole paused, shaken from the wistful moment they had just shared back into reality, with machine beeps and people crying. "I'm your nurse, Nicole. I'll be right back."

She rushed out of the room. At the nurses' desk, she searched the computer's files and discovered that Timmy had never been called. He died two years ago.

Nicole rubbed her eyes. She needed to be alone, to think. She dashed down the hall toward the staff lounge. It was empty.

She rested against the door and sighed. Grace had no one. No children. No siblings. She was even more alone than Nicole.

God, be Timmy for her this year. Be Grace's companion. And mine too.

Her shift long over, Nicole walked to her car. A light drizzle of rain fell, a few crystal droplets turning to snow on the way down. The parking lot was quiet and still.

Nothing much had changed. Nicole's car was still in the same spot where she'd left it. She waited at the stoplight the same amount of time she normally did. But Nicole sensed a subtle shifting in her heart.

The Christmas lights seemed to shine a little brighter on the drive home. The carols on the radio sounded cheerier. And the sweet fragrance of pine wafted through the front door as she entered her apartment.

Tomorrow, Grace wouldn't even remember Nicole. She wouldn't recall the hospital visit or the song they sang together. But Nicole would remember for her.

Life Application

For a while I thought I was the only one who felt alone at Christmas. But over the years, I've come to realize that everyone gets lonely at some point in their lives. God created us to want relationships that bring meaning to our lives. But our relationship with Him will always fulfill us the most.

All humans have flaws. God does not. As we wait for someone else's companionship, we can derive tremendous joy from our relationship with Him.

Throughout the Psalms, King David shares his feelings with God through heart-wrenching honesty. Psalm 73:23, 25 says, "I am always with you; you hold me by my right hand.

Whom have I in heaven but you? And earth has nothing I desire besides you."

About the Author

Rachael Landis was born on the island of Barbados. She grew up there and in Jamaica as a missionary kid. She is now working toward an associate of the arts degree for professional writing while working as a barista and a caregiver for the elderly. Her favorite things are cats, chocolate, cake, and chocolate cake. Of course, she also likes reading.

21

Guiding Star

by Sarah Earlene Shere

Joe stared at the blank computer screen, shoulders slumped. He hadn't written a single word on his Christmas assignment for the newspaper, and the deadline was two days away. He sighed. Everything he could think about regarding this holiday had already been said. What more could he add?

Needing some fresh air and hoping for inspiration, he donned a coat and stepped out into the crisp winter night. Making his way down the sidewalk, he kept alert to every sight, smell, and sound.

Lost in thought, Joe wandered into an unfamiliar neighborhood. The streetlamps here—those that were still in working order—glowed dimly. The apartments needed more than a little paint. The residents' clothes were tattered. Unkempt children played in the dirty snow.

Joe slowed when he saw a small, skinny child sitting on an

overturned metal bucket near the curb, her feet buried in a pile of trash. She shivered in her thin white dress. Her uncombed brown hair fell down around her shoulders, at times blocking her face from view.

As Joe watched from across the road, she picked up an old sheet of newspaper from the gutter. With nimble, bluish fingers she folded, turned, and tore at the paper. After letting the bulk of it fall to the ground, she unfolded the scrap remaining in her hand. Holding it up to the streetlamp, she displayed her handiwork: a doll atop a carousel horse.

A child younger than her clapped and squealed with glee, then accepted the masterpiece and scampered away.

Joe crossed the street so he could watch her more closely. A hot-drink vendor limped toward him with a smile. "Little Maria is quite an artist, isn't she?"

Joe turned. "What can you tell me about her?"

The man nodded at the girl. "She sits right there every day, making little works of art for those who pass by. Some ask her to make something specific. But those who know her best allow her to choose what to make. She always seems to know just what each person needs."

Joe's journalistic curiosity was piqued. "Where does she live?"

"She has no home or family. She gets by on donations from those who appreciate her talent." He raised an eyebrow at Joe. "Perhaps you need something that she can help you with."

What I need is a Christmas story for the paper. Was this his answer?

Enchanted by the curious scene, he drifted over to the girl and stood before her. When her lowered head lifted, he noticed her bony shoulders were slightly hunched, her small mouth twisted, and large brown eyes protruded from her pale, drawn face. Joe did not turn away from her deformities. On the contrary, he felt hypnotized as the child maintained eye contact with him.

"What do you see?" he whispered.

For a moment, the girl merely stared at him. Then she bent down and picked up a piece of newsprint from the gutter. She folded, turned, and tore at the paper till she was satisfied. Then she held out the treasure to her new admirer. "Star," she said simply, her disfigured mouth slurring the *s* a bit.

His brow furrowed.

She peered deep into his eyes. "Find star."

What did that mean?

More confused than ever, Joe went back home. At his desk, he studied Maria's delicate handiwork, impressed with its complex design.

Shaking his head, he set the star aside. He had an article to write, and he was no closer to meeting the deadline than before.

Joe decided to call it a day. He'd confront his task tomorrow with a refreshed mind.

The next morning, reinvigorated by sleep and a hot breakfast, he felt like the razor-sharp reporter of his youth, who always knew what people wanted to read and the best words with which to deliver it.

At the computer, his fingertips flew as if the article were writing itself. His readers would eat up his story about this strange, ethereal urchin!

As the sun dipped down behind the landscape outside his window, he typed his last period. With a sigh of satisfaction, Joe leaned back in his chair. Now all he needed was a picture of the tyke, and maybe a bit of an interview with her, to give that personal touch.

Joe hastened outside, eager to finish this piece. But his steps slowed when he came to the girl's usual place. He found nothing there but the overturned bucket and a pile of trash in the gutter.

He sought out the vendor and asked about Maria.

Tears welled in his eyes. "We had one of the coldest winter nights I've seen in a long time. This morning, the church caretaker found her frozen body curled up beside the manger on their front lawn. I guess the enclosure helped to block out the snow and the icy wind … but not enough."

Overwhelmed at the shocking news, Joe walked to the church. As the large stone structure came into view, he approached the life-size wooden nativity scene displayed on its front lawn. He stopped at the foot of the manger and stood there a moment, staring down at the carved image of the holy infant.

"You look troubled, brother," said a kind voice from behind him. Joe turned and saw a man about his age, with a smile and an outstretched hand. "I'm Pastor Gabe. Is there anything I can do to help?"

Joe looked back at the manger. "I just heard about the little girl who was found here this morning."

The pastor dropped his gaze. "Maria."

"You knew her?"

"My, yes. She came here every Sunday morning. The way she praised and worshipped with all her heart and soul was an inspiration to many."

Tears choked Joe's throat. "If there is a loving God, why would He allow a child to suffer on this earth and then die before she had a chance to really live?"

The pastor slowly shook his head. "God sent His Son into this dark world to release us from the curse of sin and spiritual death, which is eternal separation from Him. Through Christ's sacrifice and resurrection, we have the hope of eternal glory. There's going to be a new heaven and a new earth, where sin and death are but memories. The broken will be made whole and the weak shall be made strong."

Joe stiffened. "What does that have to do with Maria?"

"She understood the message of Christmas. Her shell was found in the manger this morning. But her soul was safe and whole in the arms of Jesus!"

Through tear-blurred eyes, Joe noticed that the star hanging over the nativity scene bore a striking resemblance to the paper creation Maria had made for him. He chuckled. "Last night she told me, 'Find star.' This is where she was directing me. This is the star she wanted me to find."

The pastor put a hand on Joe's back. "This is the Savior she wanted you to find."

Life Application

The holy babe of Christmas can still be found today … in that quiet voice that gently cries from inside humble hearts, and through the eyes of children who wonder at His birth.

Are you caught up in the wrappings of Christmas rather than the one wrapped in the manger? Have you forgotten hope in the midst of the hurry? Come, follow a star to the King of Kings, the Son of God who has been given to us.

About the Author

Sarah Earlene Shere, a Southern California native, fell in love with storytelling at the age of eleven. As she's grown closer to God and fallen in love with Jesus, her stories have become biblical and allegorical, reflecting her favorite authors, John Bunyan and Hans Christian Andersen.

Closing

As we celebrate all of our cherished holiday traditions, it's important to remember that Christmas is really about one thing—God's gift to us. The Creator of the universe sent His Son to this world, to be born as a helpless babe and live among us so He could tell us about God and heaven. Then He died, according to the Father's plan, so that sinful human beings could be made righteous in God's sight. He rose again so we can have peace and joy during our earthly sojourn as well as eternal life in heaven with the one who loves us more than we could possibly imagine.

What greater gift could there be?

But we have to accept God's perfect gift in order to enjoy the benefits. If you don't yet know Jesus in a personal way, you can start that relationship anytime. Just talk to God the same way you would a trusted friend. Tell Him you want to accept His Son into your heart. You'll never receive a better Christmas present than Jesus!

If you've been inspired or blessed by any of the stories in this book, may I encourage you to share that experience with others? Visit our website, FictionDevo.com, and find the forum on "21 Days of Christmas." Read what others are saying about the stories in this book, and post something yourself about what a particular story meant to you.

If you prefer, visit facebook.com/FictionDevo to read and write posts about all of the books in the Fiction Lover's Devotional series.

Other Books in This Series from BroadStreet Publishing

21 Days of Grace:
Stories of God's Unconditional Love
(June 2015)

21 Days of Love:
Stories that Celebrate Treasured Relationships
(January 2016)

21 Days of Joy:
Stories that Celebrate Motherhood
(April 2016)

Alphabetical List of Contributing Authors